Connor

CHRIS KENISTON

Indie House Publishing

Indie House Publishing

BOOKS BY CHRIS KENISTON

Farraday Country
Adam
Brooks
Connor
Declan
Ethan
Finn
Grace

ACKNOWLEDGEMENTS

I'm always amazed when a book finally comes together. Some books more than others! Connor was one of those challenging books.

When I was a little girl I had the good fortune to vacation in the Dominican Republic where my cousins and I learned to ride horses. Not just in an arena following horses nose to rump, but free in the hills, across untouched land and rivers. Once I even won a race! Even so, I'll be the first to admit my memories are limited and most likely only as accurate as the perceptions of a nine year old little girl. But more importantly they are not enough to write a book about a horseman.

To accomplish that I needed help from friends. Once again author JM Madden has come to my rescue. So have a handful of my fans who helped name the horses. We had fun that day on Facebook. Thank you ladies! Especially one fan in particular stepped forward with her skills at running a stable, to make sure I didn't muck things up too badly! Not only did I get Kathy Brodie's fabulous input, she brought the stable's veterinarian in on the consults! Thank you!

I hope everyone has been enjoying the Farraday brothers. Thank you all for taking the time to read my ramblings.

Enjoy!

CHAPTER ONE

"My heavens, Ralph." Still holding onto the doorknob of the upstairs bedroom, Eileen Farraday took a step back. "When was the last time you were in this room?"

Ralph Brennan, the Farraday ranch neighbor for longer than Eileen had been with the family, came to a stop beside her. "I guess a while."

"A while?" She looked over her shoulder at him. She'd walked the second floor halls of the well-kept ranch house for the first time since Marjorie Brennan passed years ago. Everything looked exactly the same, including Marjorie's sewing room and the stack of pink fabrics she'd used to make Grace's third birthday party dress. Sucking in a breath and forging forward, Eileen surveyed the remaining rooms upstairs. Dusted and clean, Marjorie would have been proud of him. Time had stood still in the Brennan house.

"I figure it's time."

Eileen's brow arched high on her forehead and out of respect for the nearly ninety-year-old man, she refrained from blurting out the first words that had come to mind, *Ya think*?

"I told Catherine I would be with her soon, but I needed to get this old house in order first. Don't want no strangers pawing through Marjorie's things."

It took Eileen a few long seconds to remember who Catherine was – the Brennan granddaughter. Eileen had never met the child, but when Ralph's wife had passed from a long bout with cancer, the little girl had been many a topic of conversation at the Farraday kitchen table. "You're going to see your granddaughter?"

The old man's smile lifted. "Yep. She's an important lawyer

where she lives in Chicago. Too hard to come to Tuckers Bluff, but I told her as soon as I get things straightened out here, I'll be heading her way for a visit."

Eileen looked down the hall. If he wanted to visit his granddaughter before the next millennium, Eileen was going to have to call in some backup. "I'll need help."

Ralph Brennan squinted. "What kind of help?"

"Extra hands. Or you won't be seeing Catherine for a long time."

"Already seen her." The man grinned at Eileen again.

"When did you leave town?" Maybe the old goat wasn't as sharp as everyone thought.

"Ain't left the ranch. Saw her on that contraption she sent me."

Contraption?

Ralph turned and walked down the stairs. Eileen figured she'd seen enough upstairs and fell into step behind him.

At the bottom of the stairs, he made a sharp right into what she knew to be his office. The room probably held records for a good fifty years or more of Brennan Ranch business—all in handwritten logs. "This thing."

Eileen chuckled, relieved the old guy wasn't losing his mind. "A computer tablet."

Ralph shrugged, then flashed a toothless grin. "She's pretty as a picture. Looks just like her mama when she smiles." He hit a switch and a photograph of what Eileen assumed was the granddaughter, now fully grown and with a young child, appeared on the screen.

"She's lovely. Hope she makes it out this way some day."

"Don't know about that. I've been waiting almost a year for that to happen and finally gave up. That's when we agreed these old bones would have to go north if we're going to visit. It's better that way for Stacey."

"The little girl?"

"Her little girl. Cute as a button." A quick frown descended over his eyes.

"What's wrong?" Eileen tread carefully. Ralph wasn't one for talking, so she knew the only way to find out what had his mood turning was to ask and then hope she hadn't stepped on any toes.

"Not sure. Little girl doesn't smile and doesn't talk. Catherine says she's just shy around new people."

"Lots of kids are that way."

"Maybe." He huffed out a ragged breath rubbed his hands together. "I wasn't too keen on leaving, but now that it's been decided, I'm rather anxious to get going. When can you get started?"

"I suppose the easiest place to start is with Marjorie's sewing room. There are lots of folks in town who could use those supplies. Maybe we'll start doing up the quilt tradition again."

"Marjorie always enjoyed making those baby quilts. Nothing made her happier than being with children. Always thought it a waste she wasn't mama to a dozen little ones, but guess the good lord thought one was enough. And late in life at that."

Eileen smiled at him. "I'm sure there were times we'd have been happy to lend you one of the boys. Or two."

"You done good with the boys. Made them right men. It does my heart good knowing this place will someday be raising Farraday children again."

"Again?"

"My great grandpappy bought this land from the first Farraday. His wife didn't like living so far away from everything. She was from some place up north, Boston maybe. Anyhow, she had a hard time adapting to the ways of a rancher, but the isolation was the hardest for her. Fearful she was going to lose her mind, he sold this land to my kin on the condition that the house be built close to the property line. That way the ladies were able to visit back and forth. Worked out just fine as both women were city girls."

"I didn't know that story." Eileen wondered how many more things the old coot had tucked away in the corners of his memory that he'd never shared. "Not much more to tell. Farradays and Brennans been neighbors ever since."

"No hidden feuds?" Eileen teased.

"Nah," Ralph shifted his weight. "Not even a bicker. My sister Edna almost ran off with Sean's Uncle George. That was fodder for the town busybodies for years. Edna was only fourteen and she and George had run off to the justice of the peace all the way in Butler Springs."

"Really?" Eileen would have to ask Sean if he knew the story. Otherwise, she knew what the topic of conversation would be at the next big Farraday reunion.

"Foolish young kids. Two years later Edna married one of the Turner boys and moved to Butler Springs. Eventually, your Uncle George met his Martha and moved to her neck of the woods. That's about all the excitement there ever was."

"Well, it sounds fun. So," Eileen clapped her hands, "why don't you find something to do, and I'll get started upstairs."

"If you don't mind, it's past my afternoon nap time. I think I'll just have a seat here and watch a little TV. Maria left a fresh pitcher of lemonade in the fridge."

"Why don't you take a seat and I'll bring us both a glass."

Ralph smiled at her. "You're a good woman, Eileen. You done right by your sister, and now you're doing right by my Marjorie."

"That's what neighbors are for, Ralph." It wasn't often anymore that the memory of her sister's life cut short so young still stung hard. Something about being in this home where time seemed to have stood still made the hurt fresher than it had been in decades. Eileen continued into the outdated kitchen. While the Farraday kitchen had been redone just before she'd arrived on the ranch, the Brennan kitchen looked like the set of a seventies sitcom. Harvest gold was the color of choice. The only sign of the modern world was the stainless steel microwave tucked away in the corner. Even the refrigerator was an ancient pull handle model, a throwback to an even earlier decade. Eileen couldn't believe the dang thing still worked. Though on second thought, it shouldn't surprise her. The fridge came from the days when appliances were built to last a lifetime, or in this case, several lifetimes. Two chilled glasses in hand, Eileen returned to the large den. "Here you go, Ralph."

His eyes closed and lips curled upward in a smile, she didn't see any reason to disturb his pleasant dream. Setting the glass down on the table beside him, an odd sensation skittered up her spine. Her heart took off in double time and she took a closer look at the peaceful smile. "Ralph," she whispered, slowly reaching for his arm. Eileen pressed two fingers on the inside of his wrist.

Closing her eyes tightly, she moved those same fingers to his neck. "Oh, Ralph."

CHAPTER TWO

Knowing the Brennan place would soon be his was just about the only thing that kept Connor Farraday from throwing this new leasehand overboard. Hand to God, that man couldn't get out of his own way. Moving a pipe through the platform of an oil rig was hard work. Moving it on a windy day was a bitch, and this kid didn't get it. He needed some time in a camp on dry land digging ditches until he learned to do what he was told, exactly as he was told, every time he was told.

At this rate Connor wasn't going to make it another day, never mind another week til the end of his rotation. Fifteen days on, seven off. He'd been pushing himself to the limit for a while, not taking the recommended full two weeks off, banking the extra pay. He'd had just about enough of this merry-go-round. Having done his time with Uncle Sam, he'd decided pretty fast that taking orders was no way to spend the rest of his life. Not for the kind of money the Marine Corps paid him. Working an oil rig, whether on land or sea, was a hard way to earn a damn good living. He'd loved the rush, the bustle, the constant challenges. A lot of guys only did this kind of work for a year or two, got their stakes, and moved on. He'd had bigger plans in mind, but it was time for the payoff.

"Put some back into it," one of the derrickhands yelled to the kid.

Getting a good look at his face, Connor spotted the sunglasses. "Where the hell are your safety glasses?"

"In my room."

Always a good place to keep protection. For half a second Connor considered asking if the guy kept his condoms in the wrapper all night. Neither one of which would do him any good when needed. "Why are you wearing sunglasses in the middle of the night?"

"They're Versace."

How did this one get past the suits and wind up Connor's responsibility? Assuming he didn't drop another screwdriver on his foot and go home crying to mama first, the kid was going to get himself killed. Or worse, if he didn't stop thinking and just do what he was told, he was going to get someone else killed too. "Go get your damn safety glasses, and if I see those sunglasses one more time it will be the last time *you* ever see them again. Understood?"

The kid may have nodded in agreement, but the look in his eyes told Connor loud and clear he didn't have a clue. If it weren't for the Brennan light at the end of the tunnel, tonight's shift would almost be enough to send Connor back to working for Uncle Sam. Idiots like this newbie weren't worth the extra pay.

Halfway through his twelve-hour shift, the sunrise this particular morning was amazing. Almost like an apology from God for making Connor put up with the dumb kid. The serene backdrop to one of the most dangerous jobs on the planet.

Below deck in the kitchen, Connor downed another energy drink, went through the line, and filled his plate. They'd worked off plenty of energy fighting the wind, he was ready to refuel.

Champing down on steak and potatoes about the same time his family back home was serving up eggs and bacon, it was no surprise when his phone sounded off with a call from his father. "Hey, Dad. What's got you calling so early in the day?"

"Thought you'd want to know, Ralph Brennan passed away yesterday."

Connor's fork froze midway to his mouth. "What happened?"

"Old age. He sat down in a chair, closed his eyes, and went to sleep. Your aunt Eileen was with him."

"She okay?"

"Yeah, he went real peaceful. Nothing she could have done for him."

"Wow. I know he was old and all that, but I didn't see this coming."

"Something else you may want to know."

When his father's voice took on that slightly lower octave, it was rarely good news. "What?"

"His granddaughter is coming to town."

"Granddaughter? The bratty kid?"

"Don't know about that, but she made arrangements with Andy over the phone. She needs time to get away, so the funeral won't be til she gets here in a week or so."

"Seems like a long way to come to say goodbye to someone you haven't had time for in . . . what, twenty, twenty-five years?"

"There is that, but she's also coming to decide what to do with the ranch."

What was left on his plate didn't look nearly as appetizing anymore. "What's there to decide? I'm buying it."

"Yeah, well." His father hesitated longer than Connor would have liked. "I know that, and you know that, and even Ralph may have known that, but it doesn't sound like the granddaughter does."

Connor pushed his half-finished plate aside. "We'll just have to see about that."

● ● ●

"Why do people always wait until it's too late?" Catherine Hammond mumbled to her assistant, Susan.

"Do you want me to answer that?" Susan looked at her with raised brows.

Returning her gaze to her desktop and the screenshot of her grandfather, Catherine shook her head. "I should have gone the first time he asked."

"You were right in the middle of the Buchanan case. There was no way you could have left without your father exploding, and frankly, Connie couldn't have handled first chair. She wasn't ready for that."

That's the same argument Catherine had given herself. It wasn't fair to Connie, the firm, and especially her father. He'd put a lot on the line the last couple of years handing her the important cases. "Still . . ."

"There was nothing you could do." Susan set a stack of requested files on the desk and retrieved another pile ready for archiving.

"I could have gone after that. I could have turned down the Medcalf appeal."

"Not if you want to make partner. You know as well as I do, if you want to play with the big boys, you can't play the family card."

If anyone knew that, it was Catherine. She'd spent a lifetime living up to her father's expectations. Work hard. Reap the rewards. No time for friends and family. And she'd worked very hard, day and night, graduating high school as valedictorian, college summa cum laude, attending University of Chicago law, and finally marrying her dad's business partner's son—all as expected.

Not that marrying David had been as much work as her other accomplishments. Much the way she'd grown up knowing she would be going to college and law school and joining Daddy's firm, she and David had grown up knowing one day they'd get married and start a family of their own. They'd been a team for as long as she could remember. A good team. Of course, her father never explained how she was supposed to fulfill both sides of that last equation, partner in the firm and mother.

"You do realize you can make all these arrangements without actually going to Texas?"

Bless Susan, she had Catherine's back twenty-four seven. Of course, Catherine always teased it was only because she was probably the first attorney in a decade who hadn't cared about Susan's hourglass figure. Susan had probably been hired for her looks, and at over forty she was a knockout by anyone's standards, but Catherine appreciated the woman's brains. Every minute of every day. "I have to go. I owe him that much."

"At least Judge Albanese likes you. It probably won't be very hard to get a continuance."

"No continuance." Catherine shook her head and stared at the screen. Her grandfather's smile haunted her already.

"Oh, good. You've come to your senses."

The bright smile that took over Susan's face didn't make it any easier for Catherine to finish her sentence. She felt an odd need to please her assistant the same way she had her father. "We're reassigning the case. I'll take the rest of the week to get . . ." she looked out the window a moment running the names of junior partners through her mind and smiled, "Connie up to speed. If she's got the chops I think she has, she's ready for first chair. This case will be career making for her."

"And breaking for you." Susan tightened her grip on the manila files. "Have you lost your mind?"

"No." Catherine shoved her chair away from the desk. "I just may have found it."

CHAPTER THREE

For the first time in a decade, bookended around his final work rotation, Connor had shared two Sunday suppers with the family in only one month.

"Pass the garlic mashed potatoes, please." Meg Farraday, Connor's new sister-in-law thanks to his brother Adam, held out both her hands to his aunt Eileen seated beside her.

Connor had been home from the rig almost five days and no one knew any more now about the fate of the Brennan ranch than they had when his father called a week ago.

"So this is it?" Meg scooped a dollop of potato onto her plate but addressed Connor. "You're home to stay."

"'Bout time," Sean Farraday said, not letting his son respond. "D.J., pass the rolls, please."

D.J., younger than Connor by two years, had also joined the Marines right out of school, done his time, and come home to roost. With a brief pit stop in Dallas on his way to becoming Tuckers Bluff's chief of police. "Here you go."

"What did the bank say?" Finn, the youngest brother, shoveled a forkful of green bean casserole into his mouth.

"Everything is in order. But to provide a letter of credit they need to do some more paperwork. According to a friend of mine, the bigger the file the happier the underwriters are. I figure I'll give them all the paper they want if it will give me what I need to finally get Capaill Stables off the ground."

"So you're staying even if the brat doesn't sell you the Brennan place?" Finn asked between mouthfuls.

And wasn't that the magic question. What the hell was Connor going to do if the granddaughter didn't want to honor the bargain he'd made with old man Brennan?

Meg wiped her mouth and set her napkin back on her lap. "I can't see why she wouldn't sell."

"She has a point." Brooks, the doctor in the family, pointed to Adam's wife. "We know the granddaughter's a lawyer in one of Chicago's most prestigious firms who hasn't been back to see her grandfather in well over twenty years."

"Twenty-five," Connor chimed in.

"Over twenty-five years," Brooks repeated. "I can't see her finding any reason not to honor the deal."

The problem as he saw it was twofold. First, she might have no interest in carrying the note for the balance of the sale price the way old man Brennan had been. The other problem was she just plain might want . . . "More money," Connor muttered, doing his best not to regurgitate the meal. "People like her are always motivated by money."

"Pot calling kettle black," Finn muttered at the other end of the table.

"That's different and you know it. Starting my own stable isn't cheap. I've been working for a stake, not cause I'm greedy."

"Who says she is?" Aunt Eileen piped up.

All eyes turned to the family matriarch.

"There's a reason," Connor answered, "that lawyers are stereotyped as bloodsucking parasites."

"So," Aunt Eileen crossed her arms. "You're saying your baby sister is a money grubbing leach?"

She would bring up that the youngest of the Farraday clan, and the only girl, was about to graduate from one of the country's top law schools. "There's always an exception or two to the rule."

"And maybe," Eileen didn't uncross her arms, "Ralph's granddaughter is an exception as well."

"Hmm," was the only sound Connor could muster. There was no sense in arguing. His aunt had a point. No one had any idea what this city woman had in mind, but he was sure of one thing—he was home to stay. All he had to figure out was where the hell that home was going to be.

• • •

What had ever made Catherine think that driving a car across barren West Texas would constitute a fun road trip? The closer she got to Tuckers Bluff, the more memories of the ranch came to the forefront of her mind. By the time she came through town, the pictures had grown sharper and now, driving under the wrought iron B overhead, she almost expected to see her grandmother sitting on the front porch snapping peas. "I wonder if Grandpa kept up the garden?"

Buckled in her booster, Stacey stared intently out the window, clutching her stuffed doggie with both hands.

"We're almost at the house, sweetie."

Stacey didn't answer.

Not that Catherine expected her to. Spotting the lone live oak tree in the front yard, her cheeks tugged at the corners of her mouth. The tire swing was still there. All these years and the tire was still there. "When I was a little girl I could play on that swing over there for hours."

In the rearview mirror, Catherine thought she saw a spark of interest in her daughter's eyes. Could the answer be something as simple as an old tire swing in the middle of nowhere? But as quickly as her eyes flashed bright, the same hollow look that had stared back at Catherine for so long reappeared.

Parked in front of the old white shiplap-sided house, Catherine had told herself not to expect to find things the same, and yet everything looked exactly as she remembered. Her grandfather had taken really good care of the place. A quick look over her shoulder and she could see her little girl taking in the surroundings with a great deal of interest. Maybe that was something. "We'd better go inside. You ready?"

Stacey blinked, but at least she turned her attention back to her mother's face. Again, baby steps. One benefit of having a child unconcerned with the world around her was that it would be a quick unloading of the car. No constant chatter with a million questions. No child tugging at her arm to go play, to explore. No need to rush to find her room and beg for a playmate. Shutting her eyes tightly closed, Catherine held back the tears. She would kill for one word from Stacey.

Inside the house smelled of roses and cinnamon. Taking in a deep breath, the familiar scents brought a new wave of memories. The house filled with the aroma of fresh baked pies, home canned jams, and coffee can bread was an everyday occurrence during her brief visits with her mom. On the days Memah wasn't baking, the house smelled of cinnamon. "Come on, Stacey."

The kitchen would have been one room Catherine would have expected to see updated for sure, but she was pretty sure nothing had changed there since before her mother was born. "Have a seat at the table and you can have a little snack while I unpack the car."

Stacey climbed up onto the Windsor chair at the end of the worn oak table, still strangling her beloved stuffed dog.

It only took a few seconds to uncover the plates and napkins. Those were also still in the same place they'd been when Catherine visited as a young child with her mom. Probably close to the same age as Stacey was now. Unzipping the small cooler, she retrieved a baggy of sliced apples and a few graham crackers. "Here you go. I'll be back in a few minutes and then…" Then what? Flooded with a monsoon of memories, Catherine didn't have the slightest idea what to do after she brought in the luggage and groceries. Instead of thinking ahead, she leaned over and kissed her baby on the top of her curly, blonde locks. At least Stacey didn't flinch at the slightest touch anymore.

Having bought only a few staples from the store in town, it didn't take long to put things away in the kitchen. She was actually surprised to find the refrigerator filled with much of what she'd already picked up as well as covered dishes with reheating instructions taped to them. She certainly wouldn't have found that if her granddad had lived in Chicago. After funeral food, sure. But a freshly stocked fridge? Unlikely.

"Now for the bags."

Stacey gnawed slowly on a graham cracker, her gaze steady out the window.

"I'll be right back. I'm going to take our bags upstairs. Okay?"

She didn't know why she asked. Stacey never spoke anymore. The occasional nod would send Catherine's heart soaring with the hope that this would be the breakthrough day, only to be disappointed. She blew out a sigh and shook her head. "Too much quiet," she mumbled to nobody. The best thing she could do was say her final goodbye to her grandfather, hire someone to help her dispose of the belongings, and get back to Chicago where she could lose herself in her work and forget everything she didn't want to remember. One more glance at the past closing in on her and she had to ask herself if maybe Susan hadn't been right. Maybe, after all she'd been through, she'd simply and unequivocally, lost her mind.

• • •

The nice thing about the days growing longer with the promise of summer was enjoying the evening air after supper. Connor's head was about to explode batting around the what-ifs at the table. He could still remember his mama's words: "If my mother had wheels she'd be a car." No arguing that one. Though it took him a long time to understand.

Pharaoh snorted and slowed to a stop, her ears pricked. Connor's gaze immediately scanned the horizon for what had caught her attention. "What the…"

Just on this side of the old fence by the Brennan property line, a fuzzy blur moved over the field. Spotting a coyote, or even a wolf, wasn't an oddity on ranch land, but the colorful little blonde blur scurrying after the four-legged critter was definitely not normal on Farraday land.

Clicking softly, and with a gentle squeeze of his heels into

Pharaoh's side, Connor shot forward, visions of a starving wolf mauling the little thing drove him and his horse to move as fast as God and nature allowed. Thundering across the pasture he struggled to pull his phone from his pocket. Every prayer he'd ever learned crossed his lips as he watched the little blonde blur move closer to the critter who had now slowed from a trot to a mere stroll. *Crap.*

Close enough to be sure he hadn't completely lost his mind and confirm the colorful blonde apparition was indeed someone's child, Connor slowed at a safe distance from the little girl and slid to his feet before Pharaoh could come to a stop. Now all he had to do was figure out how to snatch her to safety. Inching closer to avoid spooking the child or what he could now see was a snarling dog, Connor lowered his voice, "Hi there. I bet you're a long way from home."

The little girl seemed to stare past him for a moment before taking another step toward the dog who had now dropped his hind quarters. With his teeth still showing, the canine no longer in attack stance did little to reassure Connor. Though it struck him that this particular pup seemed more concerned with him than the little girl. *More for dinner.* "Good boy," he reassured the dog then, slowing his pace further, turned to the little girl. "Sweetheart, why don't you come over here with me and we'll get you home."

The little girl tilted her head slightly as though debating the pros and cons of following his instructions and then straightening herself, a glint in her eyes appeared as she took off running and closed the distance between her and the dog. *Oh God.* Bolting forward full speed, with every hurried step, Connor's mind calculated how much damage those sharp white fangs could do before he could reach the little girl.

Not til the child's wiry arms wrapped tightly around the stray dog's neck did Connor fully realize the snarling fangs were not directed at her but at him.

By the time momentum allowed him to slow to a stop, the dog was on all fours, head lowered, hackles up, and growling viciously.

The pissed-off animal was most definitely now in attack mode.

Swiping at his phone, Connor speed-dialed the house.

"Hello?"

"I'm in the north pasture just this side of Brennan's fence by the old heritage path, and I'm in a Mexican stand-off with a snarling dog and a little girl."

"A little what?" Finn Farraday said into the phone.

"You heard me. Grab a rifle and get your ass over here now. And don't spook him." Not waiting for an answer, Connor slid the phone back into his pocket and took a step closer only to have the dog's low rumble increase a notch on the vicious scale. "It's okay, boy."

Hands low, Connor retreated a step. As long as the dog was focused on him, he wouldn't have to worry about the little girl whose face was buried in the dirty fur.

"Stacey!" a panicked voice echoed from his right. "Stacey!"

Off to the side, he could see a slender figure racing across the field. "You'd better slow up," he called.

"Stacey," she screamed again. Her face blanching at the sight of the snarling animal at her little girl's side, the woman's hands rose to cover her mouth.

"Lady, ease up," he repeated. "Help's coming."

This time, the frantic woman seemed to hear him and slowed her pace, her eyes narrowing to focus on him and then turning back to the girl. "Sweetie, come here. Let the dog go and come to Mommy."

A trickle of relief touched him as the angry animal, still snarling, sat on his haunches, no longer in attack position. *Progress.*

"Stacey, baby," the woman lowered her voice, every word coming out strained with tension, "let go of the dog."

At the sound of the woman's new plea, the dog grew quiet. *Interesting.* "Ma'am. If you'll keep talking. Your voice seems to be distracting the dog. I'll try and get closer."

The woman's terrified gaze turned to him. "Don't let him hurt her."

Any other time or person and he would have snapped a colorful retort; instead, Connor nodded and silently took a careful step forward. The dog eyed him, but didn't move, didn't growl.

"Be careful," the woman whispered, clutching her hands tightly together.

Connor could feel her fear thick like a hot August day. He had to get to the little girl. In response to the female voice, the dog lowered himself to the ground and Connor paused for a second reconsidering the animal's behavior. "Ma'am, say something else. Call your daughter again."

Down on one knee, arms outstretched, the lady tried again, "Stacey, come to Mommy, dear."

Shifting his weight, the dog spread his hind legs to the side and leaned into the little girl. Did the dog understand this was her mother? Nothing else could explain the animal's change in attitude. Connor patted his side. "Good boy. Come here." Much to his surprise, the dog pushed to his feet and, easing out from under the little girl, came trotting over to Connor. "I'll be…"

"Oh, baby." Before the mother could close the distance between her and her daughter, the little girl was already running after the dog now sitting in front of Connor, tongue lolling, and tail wagging.

"So you're a protector, are you?" Connor scratched the dog's ear as the little girl arrived, throwing herself onto the pup, followed by a grateful, blubbering woman.

"Thank you. Thank you so much." The woman that he now realized was a rather attractive redhead, kissed her daughter's forehead, temple, cheek, then leaning back slightly patted the child's arms as though reassuring herself the little girl was still intact. Before he could make a move, the relieved mom shifted, flung her arms around Connor, knocked his hat off and squeezed him in a tight bear hug. "Thank you so much."

"I, uh…" Instinct kicked in. What else was a man to do when a beautiful woman landed in his arms? Especially a man who spent most of his days on an oil rig sans the company of beautiful women? His arms laced around her and the adrenaline rush that had him racing across the pasture was suddenly overpowered by a different kind of rush. The kind that would prove very embarrassing if he didn't extricate himself from her hold—and fast. Dropping his arms to his side, he sucked in a long breath and turned his thoughts to an icy swim.

Relief washed over him when she pulled back and turned her embrace on her daughter. A redhead *and* long legged. He couldn't tear his eyes away. Slowly, she released her daughter and pushed to her feet, keeping the little girl's hand clasped tightly in hers.

The girl slipped away from the mother and, casting a brief smile at Connor, wrapped herself around the dog once again.

Connor retrieved his hat and dragged his mind back to the situation at hand, a roaming little girl barely escaping the clutches of a vicious dog.

"I…I don't understand," the woman muttered, staring down at her daughter.

"You and me both, lady." Hanging on to the dog just in case, Connor met the woman's gaze. "Are you *crazy*?"

CHAPTER FOUR

None of this made any sense to Catherine. Stacey didn't just wander off. She played with her toys, watched a little TV, and on occasion tinkered with Catherine's phone or tablet. Chasing dogs and smiling at strange men—even handsome ones—was simply not the norm. Not anymore.

"It isn't safe to let kids run loose on other people's pastures. You're just damn, er darn, lucky we didn't have cattle or horses feeding here today." The man stared her down, his hands maneuvering along the dog's neck and rubbing under his chin.

Did dogs have chins? "She must have seen your dog from the kitchen window. Followed him." The panic at not finding Stacey in the kitchen began to ebb slowly, and in its place, sheer fury bubbled at the danger her daughter could have been in. All over an unleashed dog. Straightening to her full height, Catherine turned on the good-looking cowboy. "*You* really shouldn't let a vicious animal run loose."

"He doesn't seem all that vicious now." The cowboy continued stroking the dog. "And he's not my dog."

The big furry animal lifted a paw onto the stranger's legs, and Catherine arched one brow. "Could have fooled me."

Pounding hooves actually shook the ground beneath her. Looking up, she saw two horses coming straight for them, and like a close up on an old TV western, the horses still seemed to be moving as the riders hopped off the side and, landing on their feet, ran toward the crouching cowboy.

"This is the vicious animal?" The younger of the two approaching men tucked a pair of gloves into his back pocket and laughing hovered behind the other cowboy.

"Zip it, Finn."

The taller of the two newly arrived men seemed very intent on the dog, his eyes quickly scanning the animal from head to toe. "It's him again."

"Again?" The cowboy still petting the dog asked.

The guy who looked to be as tall as a palm tree responded, "The one who cornered Toni's husband."

That did so not sound very good. If Catherine hadn't seen the snarling animal for herself, she never would have believed that the dog now snuggled up beside her daughter could be mean to anyone. Good manners suddenly sprang to life. She could sort this all out after she introduced herself. Sticking her hand straight out to the taller man, she said, "I'm Catherine Hammond."

Both men who'd arrived on horseback nodded and tipped their hats. She supposed that was the Texas equivalent of a handshake.

When she didn't let her hand fall, the taller was the first to reach out. "Adam Farraday. Pleased to meet you."

From behind him, the younger one followed suit. "Finnegan Farraday, ma'am."

Still crouching by the dog, the man who thought her to be crazy only stared at her with piercing blue eyes that stood out in colorful contrast to his sun-darkened skin. The difference between earning your tan the hard way through ranch work and paying for it. Not till Adam kicked him lightly in the behind did he speak, "Connor Farraday."

She remembered the ranch next door had boys. A faint memory of one of them being sort of nice to her tickled the back of her mind, but for the most part, all she remembered was hating the ranch, the horses, and the boys who picked on her mercilessly for not knowing how to do anything.

Pushing to his feet, the cowboy with the bright blue eyes kept his hand on the dog's head. "You're Ralph's granddaughter?"

"I am."

"We're sorry for your loss," The tall one removed his hat and the younger brother did the same, dipping his chin in agreement.

"Well, thank you for your help." Catherine wasn't sure what else to say. For most of her life she'd thought her grandparents were already dead. "Come on, baby."

Rather than go with her mom, Stacey clung to the ratty, old dog. Her cheek on his back, her gaze off in the distance where the horses stood.

"Sweetie. We have to give this man back his dog."

"He's not—"

Catherine cut her daughter's rescuer off with a glare that would make a Supreme Court justice reconsider his words. Good thing for this cowboy he caught on quick.

"We have to go," she repeated more sternly. Leaning over she pulled Stacey's arms from the dog and tugged her daughter onto her hip. After almost two years of virtual silence and near-total acquiescence, a temper tantrum about now would have been surprisingly appreciated. Instead, leaning her cheek on her mama's shoulder, Stacey merely curled into Catherine.

"You'll be letting us know if you need anything," the taller one, Adam, called to her as she turned her back to him.

"Thank you," were the only words she could muster. The kind of help she needed, no one could give.

• • •

Connor and his brothers kept their eyes on their new neighbor's back as she carried the small girl away.

"It's a long walk to Brennan's house." Finn pulled his gloves from his pocket.

"She didn't strike me as wanting to stick around while one of us went for an ATV." Adam carefully watched the woman unlatch the old gate and walk through. "Wonder what's wrong with the kid?"

The same exact thought had just passed through Connor's mind. He hadn't noticed the little girl's silence right away. At first, he'd been seriously ticked-off at the lady for allowing her kid to wander off in unfamiliar territory, especially a city kid who didn't have the first clue about how dangerous large ranch animals could be just because of their sheer size. Then he'd been flummoxed by the wave of heat from her nearness. Once he'd gotten his head out of his ass, he'd gone back to being furious for her not keeping a better eye on the cute kid.

"Do you think she's just shy?" Finn turned toward his horse. "Where did he go?"

Dragging his gaze away from the empty pasture, Connor redirected his attention on his brother and seeing his horse exactly where Finn had left him, pointed at the gelding. "He's right there."

"Not Ace. The dog."

Adam and Connor both spun in place, scanning to the left then right.

"Son of a …" Hands shading his eyes, Adam pivoted from side to side again searching the distance. "Definitely has to be the same dog. He did it again."

"Did what?" Connor was clearly lagging behind on the dog thing.

"Disappeared." Adam shook his head. "It was too dark to get a good look at him out on the road the morning I found Meg stranded outside the Thomas Ranch, but it sure looks like the dog that had Toni's scumbag husband cornered."

"Yeah, well, if he was as protective of Toni as he was just now with Stacey, then it sounds like the same dog to me." Connor adjusted his hat for something to do with his hands.

"What I don't get," Adam turned on his heel again, "is where the hell does that animal keep coming from? Who does he belong to?"

"Looks like another one of those questions for heaven." Finn placed the toe of his boot in the stirrup and swung his leg over the back of his favorite horse. Settled in the saddle, he tugged on the reins. "See you back at the house. Aunt Eileen is going to want to know Ralph's granddaughter is here."

Adam clicked for his horse. "I'm surprised you didn't say

anything about buying the ranch."

"Wasn't the time." Truth was buying the ranch next door hadn't even entered his mind. The fight-or-flight adrenaline rush that had shot into the stratosphere at the sight of a wild canine and innocent child cleared his mind of every thought but one, saving the little girl. Not that it appears now she needed saving. He didn't even want to think about where his mind had gone when she'd flung herself at him. So didn't want to go there. The instant spark was nothing more than a chemical reaction. It had been a while since he'd enjoyed a woman's company. There wasn't anything special about this woman. Nothing at all.

"You still with us?" Adam sat high on his favorite horse. "Are you going to camp out here or come back to the house?"

"House," Connor mumbled, walking to where Pharaoh stood waiting for him. Now that he knew who he would be dealing with, it was time he found out what he was up against.

CHAPTER FIVE

"Four ladies. Read 'em and weep." Eileen Callahan spread her cards on the table. The moment the Tuckers Bluff Ladies Afternoon Social Club heard that Ralph Brennan's granddaughter was back in town, a Monday morning poker game was called to order.

Sally May tossed down her cards with a groan. "Even with Nora missing a weekday game for work, I can't seem to catch the hot seat. That's three weeks in a row you've been on a winning streak."

"And I'm a whopping four dollars and twenty cents richer in funny money." Eileen stacked her chips to her side. They'd been playing penny poker for almost as long as she'd lived in Tuckers Bluff. Using the colored poker chips made them feel like big time players, but no one was going to get rich or go broke playing cards at the Silver Spur Café.

"I'm not surprised that child turned out to be a looker." Ruth Ann dealt the cards and returned the conversation to the reason the game had been convened. "I remember Catherine being the prettiest little thing. Marjorie was so proud of her. The kid inherited Marjorie's smile from her mama."

"Is she still a carrot top?" Sally May asked.

Eileen shrugged. "If you mean a flaming red head like Meg, no. More of an auburn. Definitely not brown. Nice red highlights. Reminds me of a sorrel."

"Just what every woman wants, to be compared to a horse." Ruth Ann tossed a chip into the pot. "I'm in."

"And she didn't give you any hint of what she's doing here or how long she's going to stay?" Sally May asked.

"Nope." Eileen anted up. "We only spoke a few minutes after

I dropped off the pie—"

Dorothy looked up from her cards. "Blueberry sour cream?"

"No," Eileen laughed. "You know whenever I make those you get one. Apple crumb."

Dorothy returned her attention to the cards in her hand with a smile. "Just checking."

"So all we know is," Ruth Ann set two cards on the table, "that she's pretty, she's got a young daughter, and she's tired after a long trip from Chicago?"

"Not much more than we already knew when Andy announced he was instructed to hold off on the services until the granddaughter could arrive." Dorothy discarded three cards.

"I don't think she knows what she's doing yet either." Eileen slipped her new cards into her hand one at a time. "I mentioned that I'd agreed to help Ralph dispose of Marjorie's things and would be glad to follow through with that."

"What did she answer?" Sally May asked

"That she'd let me know."

"Sounds like a polite no to me." Looking at her cards, Dorothy held back a smile.

Eileen shook her head. "I don't think so. She was still pretty shook up after little Stacey ran onto our property chasing after that wild dog."

Ruth Ann and Sally May pulled their cards close to their breast and stared up at Eileen like a pair of matching bookends. Dorothy folded her cards and put one hand on her hip. "You're just getting around to telling us there's a pack of wild dogs around?"

"Not a pack. One. And not that kind of wild." Eileen huffed. "According to the boys, he was real protective of the little girl, snarling at Connor and not leaving Stacey until her mother got there."

"Sounds like he'd make a good ranch dog." Sally May resumed studying her cards. "Just needs a family to love him."

Resorting her cards, Eileen shook her head again. "Nope. This guy, or girl, is a loner. Disappears as fast as it appears."

"You've seen it before?"

"Same one that cornered Toni's jerk of a husband."

"Nice doggy." Sally May tossed a chip in the pot. "I'm in for five."

"Speaking of troubled husbands." Ruth Ann looked over the top of her cards at the ladies. "Have any of you noticed what's going on with Charlotte and Jake Thomas?"

Eileen kept her focus on the cards. She'd promised Brooks and Adam when she'd overheard them talking about the situation that she wouldn't spread any gossip. But she didn't say she wouldn't listen.

"You mean the broken wrist?" Dorothy asked.

"Maybe." Frowning, Ruth Ann shifted her cards. "Burt Larson says that young Jake exploded at Charlotte in the feed store yesterday, she got really quiet, and Jake escaped to the back room just before Burt intervened."

"I wonder if that explains why D.J.'s been frequenting the feed store a little more than usual," Sally May said.

"I'm out." Ruth Ann set her cards down. "I don't know. Mrs. Peabody was yacking away at the Cut and Curl about how when she'd been in to pick up some seed for her birdfeeders, Jake blew up at Jim Brady. Jake's wife had to step in and finish the sale when he went out back to cool off."

Eileen set her cards down. "He got upset with a customer?"

"Tess Rankin was getting her hair done that day and said the same thing happened to her. Jake seemed confused about her husband's order and then snapped at her as if it were her fault he didn't know what he was doing. Said it was bound to happen. Any offspring of old man Thomas couldn't stay a nice guy forever."

"I think," Dorothy tossed a matching five chip into the pot, "we need to step up the hospitality committee. Keep an eye on Charlotte Thomas. We can't be those people who see something's wrong and do nothing."

And wasn't that the truth. But from what Brooks had told Eileen about the day he'd set Charlotte's wrist, the woman insisted her husband was a kind and loving man. How the heck does a person help someone blinded by love?

• • •

Up before dawn to help Finn with ranch work, Connor had spent the better part of the day sweating out his frustrations. He loved working the land with his family, but he lived to work with horses. Anyone who had ever spent even a short while with those massive tender-hearted beasts understood how he felt. He knew a handful of people who would probably be more than happy to sell him the acreage needed for what he wanted to do. If not in this county than the next one over. But that wasn't original Farraday land.

The pull of the neighbor's land was the proximity to his family. Though he wasn't thinking of marrying and raising a family now, it was always understood that someday, like Adam, all the brothers would find the right woman and settle down. Connor buying enough of the Brennan place for his quarter horse operation and Finn picking up the rest for the Farraday Cattle Company made sense. Recently learning that the Brennan's land had originally been Farraday land made it providential.

Pulling himself together by the proverbial bootstraps and reaching out to Catherine Hammond was the best way to find out where he stood and stop stewing over what-ifs. Riding up to the old Brennan house, Connor dismounted and dropped the reins, leaving Pharaoh ground tied under the lone oak tree for shade. He wasn't facing a firing squad. Squaring his shoulders, he took his first step as the front door squeaked open.

The little girl in the doorway was cute as a button. With each tentative step, her blonde curls bounced in the sunlight. In the moment yesterday evening, he'd been more focused on the dog than the girl. And then the mother. He wasn't an expert by any sense of the word, but if he were going to guess, he'd venture the kid was around four or five. Though, shouldn't five-year-olds talk your head off? Wearing a pair of dark tights and a flowery blue dress, she looked very much the city girl. The few kids he knew wore jeans and boots, just like the grownups, from before they could walk. The colors brought out the bright blue of her eyes. They matched her mother's.

Nearly in front of her, he crouched down, not wanting to startle her with his height. Kids weren't his strong suit, but no Farraday son made it through years of Sunday services without learning a thing or two about dealing with the village of children who descended in town on potluck Sundays. "Hello again. Remember me?"

Unlike yesterday the little girl nodded and he considered that a good sign. Maybe today's conversation with her mother would be better than yesterday. Almost immediately her gaze diverted over his shoulder to where Pharaoh gnawed on what little grass there was.

"You like horses?"

The little girl didn't respond, she merely sidestepped and headed for the horse.

Pulling up to his full height, he reached out to her. "If you're going to approach a ranch horse, you'll need to hold my hand. Is that okay?"

She didn't nod or speak but accepted his hand.

Even though he knew she was just a child, the smallness of her hand in his still took him by surprise and sent an oddly protective wave racing through him. This little girl certainly didn't take after her mother when it came to horses. No fear in her eyes, she practically pulled him forward. Once they'd come close to Pharaoh, he slowed his steps. "Okay, sweetie, I'm going to pick you up so you can reach the horse's head. Is that all right with you?"

The head of blonde curls bobbed rapidly and Connor smiled. She may be shy, but she liked horses and that made her a star in his book. Hefting her up with his left arm, he stopped in front of Pharaoh.

"Here's what you do, always approach a horse from right

about here so he can see you. Unlike people, horse's eyes are on the side of their heads. You don't want to spook them by coming at them from in front. Do you understand?"

The little head bobbed again.

"Good." He ran his right hand down the side of Pharaoh's head. "Pet him nice and easy like I just did."

Without any hesitation, she leaned slightly forward and brushed her hand down the side of the horse's face, pausing at the edge of his jaw for an extra rub and then started over again.

An odd burst of satisfaction filled his chest, much like the sense of pride that had filled him from head to toe when his sister Grace had taken the prize on a horse he'd raised and trained. "That's the way."

Stacey lowered her head, looking down at her hand. Pharaoh's soft nose gently nuzzled her palm, his whiskers most likely tickling the sensitive skin. A wary smile spread briefly across the young child's face before she flung herself forward and wrapped her small arms around the large animal's neck.

Spreading his feet for balance, Connor tightened his hold on Stacey. "Easy. Remember we don't want to spook him."

Not that it mattered. Pharaoh continued to nuzzle against Stacey, eager to return the affection.

"I'll be a…"

"What are you doing!" Catherine Hammond's angry voice boomed across the yard.

CHAPTER SIX

Twice in two days was too much. First a temperamental stray dog and now this. A horse. A damn killer horse. "Get away from that animal." Catherine stomped across the front yard at a brisk trot, her heart racing twice as fast. Who knew coming to Texas would be so dangerous for her daughter. "Please."

The cowboy from yesterday, Connor, took a reactive step back but, just like with the dog last night, Stacey had her arms around the neck of another animal. A horse big enough to trample a grown man to death.

"Let's go see your mama," Connor cooed softly to Stacey, tugging gently at her elbow.

Stacey slowly slid her arms away, her gaze still fixed on the horse. Once again Connor tried to retreat and Stacey gave the horse a last minute kiss, and then smiling, flung her arms around Connor's neck.

The unexpected sight of an almost happy child robbed Catherine of all her bluster. Her steps slowed, her mouth went dry, and she was almost blinded by her daughter's bright grin. Almost two years without a single smile and now not one, but two big grins in less than twenty-four hours. What Catherine couldn't decide was if the smiles were for the animals or the cowboy.

Untethered from Stacey's hold on the massive animal, Connor turned toward Catherine. His gait was slow and easy and he walked as though carrying a young child was nothing new to him. Oddly enough it wasn't the blue eyes sparkling at her, or the hard-earned muscles, or the dark curls peeking out from under that white-knight Stetson that made him look sexy as hell. What made him a hundred times more handsome than how he'd looked the night before was the huge smile on her little girl with her arms wound happily around his neck.

Face to face in the middle of the yard, Connor squatted to set Stacey on the ground. "We didn't mean to upset you. Pharaoh is as gentle as they come. Stacey could crawl around his legs and he wouldn't move. She'd be perfectly safe."

Yeah, right. Catherine stretched out her arm, hand open, silently calling her daughter to her side, a little surprised when Stacey hesitated a moment. Though considering all the other odd reactions that this cowboy and ranch country had drawn from her daughter, the hesitation shouldn't have come as a surprise at all.

Her daughter safely tucked at her side, Catherine addressed the man before her. "If you're coming to scold me again—"

"No, ma'am." Connor tipped his hat. "Shall we agree to chalk up yesterday's words to a mutual concern for Stacey?"

"Fair enough." She could agree to that even if it didn't account for the unexpected rush of sensations that had caught her off guard when she'd found herself wrapped in his arms. "Thank you for being there to rescue my daughter."

"In hindsight, I don't think she was ever really in danger."

"Maybe." Catherine agreed politely, but the snarling dog's white fangs had become a constant image in the back of her mind. One mistake, one wrong move, and she could have lost her baby, this time for real. But that wasn't this man's fault. It was her fault for leaving Stacey unattended in the kitchen while she unpacked the car. "Would you like to come in for something to drink? Your aunt left me stocked with enough food and drink to feed the town."

Connor chuckled. The laugh looked good on him. "Thank you. I'd like that."

Leading the way, she crossed over the threshold and sucked in a soft breath. Each time she entered the old ranch house it was as if she'd stepped back in time. And each time was just as startling as the one before. "Please have a seat anywhere you'd like. I'll get us a glass of lemonade." She waved her arm across the large den that worked as both family room and living area.

"No need to go to all that trouble. A glass of water would be just fine."

"No trouble at all. Your aunt left a full pitcher. I don't think I remember ever having real lemonade."

"Your grandmother made the best strawberry lemonade this side of the Rio Grande." Rather than sit, he followed Catherine into the kitchen. "Spring is a busy time at a ranch. Sometimes when your grandpa was short-handed, Dad would bring us boys over to help Mr. Brennan with whatever cattle chores were needed. Your grandmother always rewarded us with a double slice of whatever pie she'd made and a tall glass of strawberry lemonade. She used to tease that she hid a lemon tree in the attic."

"I wish I had stronger memories of her. Walking around this house I see flashes of a woman. Hints of a memory that doesn't quite come into focus, but I know would be a good memory."

Connor nodded. "Miss Marjorie was a nice lady. We were all sorry when she passed."

"Do you know what she died from?"

Hat in hand, Connor fiddled with the brim. "I was young at the time so I don't really know, but some say it was a broken heart."

Catherine nodded. All she knew from her grandfather was that Memah had gone to sleep one night not long after her seventy-first birthday and never woke up. It was almost ironic that both her grandparents had more or less passed away in the same manner. Closing their eyes never to open again. No pain, no trauma, just a restful end. "The one thing that gives me a touch of comfort is knowing the first thing Grandpa would see when he opens his eyes again is our lord, and then my grandmother. I could tell he still missed her."

"Aunt Eileen mentioned you'd reconnected with Mr. Brennan."

Again, Catherine bobbed her head. "He was supposed to come visit us. I was too busy to come here." She bit back a bitter smile. "I couldn't find the time to come see him while he was still alive, but here I am when it's too late."

"I think it would make him happy to know you're here."

"I'm not sure what I expected to find, but I knew I had to come."

This time, Connor nodded. There wasn't really much he could say to that.

Stacey had already established herself at the head of the table with a coloring book and crayons when Catherine gave her a glass of lemonade and then set one down for her guest before pouring herself another.

"So." She took a seat at the table across from Connor. "What brings you over today?"

• • •

Suddenly asking her intentions about the property after talking about her grandparents' passing didn't seem like the best idea Connor had ever had. And yet, putting this off much longer wasn't going to make it any easier, especially with him not knowing how long she'd be staying. "How much do you know about your grandfather's plans for this place?"

"I know he's leasing the pastures to your family for grazing."

Connor nodded. "That's right. Sold us his cattle when Finn graduated from school and came to work full time on the family ranch. A couple of the cowhands came with them."

"Did he say why he sold out?"

"Your grandfather was a strong man into his old age, but ranching is hard work for young men. I think once he couldn't go out there and sink fence posts or wrestle a feisty calf himself anymore, there was no point in carrying on."

The woman stared down at her untouched glass. "Did you know I thought they were dead?"

"Excuse me?" He wasn't following. They were both gone.

"When Mama died I was six years old. Dad tried to explain to me what happened but at that age, you have no concept of mortality. For the longest time. I kept expecting Mama to come home, even though Daddy had said she'd gone to heaven. I figured it was like visiting Texas and she could come back whenever she wanted."

"I'm sorry." The pain of losing his own mother at what should have been such a happy time for the Farradays, the birth of the long awaited little girl, the one his mother was so anxious to share girly things with, stung as sharply now as it had twenty-five years ago. Though perhaps growing up on a ranch made him more capable of understanding the circle of life. They'd lost plenty of ranch animals, and Connor understood too well when his mother died that she was most definitely not boarding an airplane and coming home again. "I was nine when my mother died."

Catherine lifted her eyes to his, her gaze steady, soulful, compassionate. "I'm sorry for your loss." She ran her finger around the rim of her glass. "Do you remember a lot about her?"

"Yeah," he smiled. "I do. Not as much as Adam. He was twelve. I'll always remember her."

"I remember snatches of images. In my room reading before bedtime. Sitting at her vanity slathering on lotion. Pretty music when she played the piano."

"They sound like nice memories."

She nodded. "But they're fading more and more. I don't even remember what she really looked like. More of a collage of colors. Dark hair, fair skin, blue dress."

"Surely you have photographs? Each of us boys got to pick our favorite photo of our mother then Dad put them in frames he thought mom would have liked and set them at our bedside. That way when we said our goodnights, we could say goodnight to Mom too. Just like before."

Catherine made a scoffing noise at the base of her throat. "My father threw out every single photograph of my mother. All her belongings. Even her jewelry was sold."

"He didn't save anything for you?"

Her head turned from side to side. "It was almost as if she'd never existed."

"Does this have something to do with you not visiting your grandparents anymore?"

"From what I gathered from my grandfather, very much so. After Mom died, Dad packed us up and moved us to Chicago and I never saw or heard from Mama's parents again. I guess I thought when she died, they died."

"The family plan," he mumbled to himself.

"I can't imagine the pain of losing a daughter and for all intents and purposes, a granddaughter as well." Catherine stared at the little girl whose attention was riveted on the scribbled paper.

The extent of her father's actions suddenly dawned on him. She hadn't chosen not to come; she didn't know she had somewhere to go. And as for Old Man Brennan... " Your father didn't tell them what happened, where you were."

"No." She raised her gaze to meet him. "And two old people didn't understand how to use resources to find out why. You have no idea how shocked I was to receive his letter."

Connor could only imagine.

"I finally got that connection to my mother that had been cut off too young, only to lose that as well."

The words I'm sorry rolled to the tip of his tongue, but he held them back. He was pretty sure she didn't want his pity. "Have you and Stacey had dinner yet?"

"No." Her gaze bounced to the old kitchen clock on the wall. "I decided to start going through Grandad's office first. I didn't realize it's getting to be that time."

"Good, then. Aunt Eileen cooks enough food to feed a small army. Please join us for supper?"

"Oh, I wouldn't want to impose. Your aunt left me plenty—"

"Please come. I think any one person can only take so much walking down memory lane on their own before they need the insanity of an Irish family to make them realize how truly sane their world really is."

A hint of a smile graced her lips and Connor felt a burst of pleasure at having helped put it there. Besides, if she was going to tell him that she wasn't keeping her grandfather's bargain, he didn't want to hear it just yet.

CHAPTER SEVEN

"She's driving over now." Connor pulled his aunt into the circle of his arms and kissed the top of her head. Eileen Callahan was a petite woman compared to her nephews. Only an inch shorter than Adam and Brooks, Connor towered over his aunt and loved the way she giggled whenever he twirled her like a ballerina before enveloping her in a Texas-size hug. "I figured you wouldn't mind."

"Well, of course, I don't." Just like she'd done when they were growing up, she patted his cheek with her hand and then tugged him down so she could kiss the other cheek. "The more the merrier. Besides, even though she's grown apart from her mom's kin, I can see the deep hurt at losing Ralph."

"Did you know that her father cut her off from the Brennans after her mother died?"

Eileen shook her head. "No, but I knew something was up. Ralph wouldn't say an unkind word about a rattlesnake, but from what little he'd said the few times he opened his mouth, I had a feeling it was something like that. Especially since no woman who had chosen to ignore her grandparents as a child and remained out of touch for decades, suddenly sends her grandfather a tablet to do video chats with."

"No. I suppose not." Connor lifted the lid on a simmering pot. "Damn, I missed your cooking. The rigs serve really good meals, but it's not the same."

Eileen's cheeks flushed slightly pink. With her Irish complexion, it didn't take much to make her blush, and any compliment from her boys was always a sure fire guarantee that she would, but he hadn't expected to see moisture pooling in her eyes. "I'm glad you're home. You've been missed."

Before he could pull her into another hug, she spun away from him and stirred the simmering sauce.

"Well, that smells like it will hit the spot." Sean Farraday came down from showering and changing for supper after a long day's work. Even though Finn seemed to be making more and more decisions about the direction the ranch management was going, Sean Farraday was still head of the Farraday clan and the Farraday ranch.

More than twenty-five years of affection passed between the smiles and nods, and Aunt Eileen spoon-feeding his dad a taste of the casserole sauce. Connor wondered how different that scene would be if his mother were still alive. Somewhere in the back of his mind, he could still remember walking into the kitchen and finding his parents wrapped in a heated embrace. Not that he'd realized just how heated it was at the time, but he certainly understood how they'd wound up with seven children in rapid succession.

"You better set the table for an extra two places," Eileen said to Connor.

Sean glanced at the four place settings at one end of the massive oak kitchen table. Once upon a time, there had been seven boisterous children, two overly patient adults and for a while his own father at the table. Connor could almost see the memories passing across his father's eyes like a motion picture. "Who we expecting?" his dad asked.

"Catherine and her little girl," Eileen said.

Connor's dad nodded. "Good. Good. I'll be in my office until they arrive."

Setting down the spoon, Eileen waved a free hand at Sean and, returning her attention to the stove, poured the creamy liquid over a deep dish of chicken and ham.

The front doorbell sounded.

"That must be them. No one else around here would ring the bell." Aunt Eileen shoved the casserole into the oven, slammed it shut, and quickly wiped her hands on a dishrag. "Hurry up now. Don't want them growing roots on the front porch."

Connor bit back a smile. He really was happy to be home. Even though his job was weeks on and weeks off, in an effort to save more money during the off time, he'd take on jobs closer to the rigs and rarely come home. But not anymore.

The door swung open and Catherine stood in a button-down, loose-fitting lilac blouse with a simple black skirt and pointy shoes that didn't belong anywhere on a ranch. "I thought I'd freshen up for dinner."

Her sweet smile made up for the poor choice in footwear, and Connor decided telling her that she looked plenty fresh half an hour ago was probably not appropriate, so instead he smiled back and led the two into the living room.

Stacey stood close to her mom, but her eyes scanned the walls and ceilings, and at the sound of Finn stomping down the stairs, her head turned to follow his steps.

"Hello again," Finn smiled at Catherine for a few seconds longer than made Connor happy—which made no friggin' sense—before Finn squatted to greet Stacey. "It's nice to see you again."

Stacey didn't say anything. Other than her gaze meeting Finn's, she didn't actually acknowledge he'd said anything at all.

"She's a bit… bashful," Catherine explained away.

"Hmm." Finn pushed to his feet and tossed a glance in Connor's direction. His eyes repeating the same question he'd posed last night. What was going on with the little girl?

"Welcome to our home." Coming from his office, Sean Farraday walked into the room and offered a welcoming grin to their neighbor's long lost granddaughter. "I do say you grew up nicely. Ralph would be proud."

Stacey stepped closer to her mom's legs, almost hiding behind her.

"And you, young lady, are as pretty as your mama was at your age," Sean's smile widened for the little girl.

Considering the older man's words, little Stacey must have

deemed them acceptable as she took a tentative step out from behind her mother to examine Sean Farraday more closely.

Doing nothing more than smiling, Sean waited for the young child to finish her perusal before straightening and guiding everyone further into the living room. "Have a seat. Can I fix anyone a drink? Bourbon, whiskey, wine?"

Finn shook his head. Connor too. While a cool drink often hit the spot, liquor was something most of the brothers relegated to a night out on the town or a celebration of some kind.

"I've got a nice bottle of pinot grigio in the fridge." Aunt Eileen joined them. "Can I tempt you?"

"Well." Catherine looked at the people in the room, Sean had just finished pouring himself a short glass of bourbon on the rocks. "Yes, thank you, that would be very nice."

Drinks served, supper in the oven, and a little time to kill, the family chatter began. There was some talk of the weather being especially mild this season, one of the feed trucks breaking down, and separating the cattle this morning for shots. "Went pretty quick having the extra hands," Finn looked to his brother.

Connor set his ankle across his knee. "Glad to be here, little brother."

"How many brothers are there?" Catherine asked.

"Six brothers. One sister." Eileen took a sip of her wine.

"Oh, my." Catherine quickly scanned the few brothers in the room.

Sean Farraday laughed. "Yeah, that about covers all I can say in mixed company."

The comment made Catherine chuckle and Connor was inexplicably contented that she'd taken it in the good graces with which it had been intended. Too often he found city girls considered a Texan's way of treating a lady more of an offense than an honor. Somehow simple respect was perceived as belittling—a good reason he intended to stay away from big cities and their women.

Eileen shifted forward in her seat. "How are you finding the house so far?"

Sean lowered his drink halfway to his lips. "Eileen, she's only been here a day."

"So?" Eileen frowned at her brother-in-law. "I only needed ten minutes to know I never wanted to set foot in Los Angeles ever again."

"Don't like big cities?" Catherine asked.

"Oh, I love them. But Los Angeles is more like visiting a smokehouse. I started coughing within hours and didn't stop until I breathed fresh air again."

Catherine chuckled softly. "The air does seem pretty fresh around here." She looked to Stacey who, clutching her stuffed dog, Woof, had shifted to sit on a nearby low stool and watch the conversation.

"You're from Chicago, correct?" Sean asked.

"I was born in Philadelphia, but for the most part raised in Chicago."

"The Windy City." Sean smiled. "Will your husband be joining you?"

Catherine's eyes sparked with surprise. "Uh, no. He passed away a couple of years ago."

Sean glanced over at the little girl. "Sorry for your loss."

Heads bobbed around the room as a moment of awkwardness settled around them.

Grabbing a dish of nuts from the nearby coffee table, Aunt Eileen came to her feet and smiling, held the dish out to Catherine. "What do you do in Chicago?"

"I'm an attorney at my father's law firm."

"My daughter is in her last year of law school at SMU in Dallas." Sean tipped his glass at his guest. Everyone in the room seemed more at ease with the new direction of conversation.

"Really?" Catherine's voice lifted, apparently the Dallas school carried some weight in Chicago, too. "And she's going to work around here?" The approval in her voice twisted into something between disbelief and disdain.

Aunt Eileen's expression fell. "Not likely." Anything else she might have added was interrupted by the squeak of the front door opening.

Catherine stiffened slightly, but no one else in the room budged. This wasn't the sort of place where ill-intending strangers invaded.

"Hey, didn't recognize the car outside." D.J.'s voice carried from the short entry. "I tried calling to say I was barging in on supper but no one—"

Standing in full uniform under the den archway, D.J.'s words were cut off by little Stacey shooting to her feet and belting one blood-curdling scream. The child took off running. Straight into Connor's arms.

● ● ●

It took Catherine a moment to put all the pieces together. While screaming cries in the middle of the night were fewer and farther apart, this was the first time Stacey had made any sound in waking hours since the accident. Muttering to herself, she tore her gaze away from her little girl curled up in a stranger's arms, her head buried in his shoulder.

The way Connor patted her back and cooed comforting words, anyone would have thought they were father and daughter.

"I'm sorry," Catherine looked to D.J. "I think it's the uniform."

Eyes wide, D.J. took a step back and bounced his attention from the terrified child to her mother. "I...uh." He retreated another step.

Aunt Eileen jumped to her feet. "Don't just stand there. Let's get you into the other room and out of that shirt. It's probably the badge."

Already walking toward her daughter, Catherine nodded at the woman's good sense. "Stacey's so bashful and ... a little intimidated by...uniforms. I really am sorry."

"No need to apologize," Sean said, focusing on his son and the child in his arms. Concern clearly etched in the elder Farraday's face.

"Sweetie," Catherine brushed a lock of hair behind her daughter's ear; then, sliding her hands under Stacey's arms, tugged her daughter away from Connor and into her own embrace. "It's okay. Nothing's wrong."

She caught the curious glance Mr. Farraday and the remaining sons exchanged. She wasn't about to go into all the changes she and Stacey had gone through. The hiccup of a dissipating sob stabbed at Catherine. What she wouldn't give to take this pain away from her little girl. To go back in time, leave work early, and pick Stacey up at daycare that day instead of having David pick her up.

Aunt Eileen slowly inched her way closer to the huddle. "I know we haven't had supper yet, but I bet a little taste of dessert would be all right."

Stacey kept her face buried in her mama's shoulder.

"Apple pie?" Aunt Eileen coaxed.

No movement from Stacey.

"With vanilla ice cream?" Aunt Eileen moved closer.

"Your favorite," Catherine added.

Stacey moved her head to see the older woman coming toward her with a smile.

"Maybe with a little chocolate sauce too?" Eileen said.

Chocolate sauce was the key. Stacey lifted her head and sucked in a long, ragged breath, stifling the last remnants of the short crying jag, and shimmied off her mother's hip, but instead of following Aunt Eileen as Catherine had expected, Stacey stuck out her hand to Connor.

Connor's face reflected the surprise Catherine felt. Slowly, he folded his hand around Stacey's and led her to the kitchen.

While Eileen scurried after the pair, Sean Farraday made no effort to move. Brows buckled with concern, he turned his attention to Catherine. She could see his mind processing the scene, working his thoughts.

The man took a step back. "Whatever is going on with you and your daughter may be none of my business, but I owe a great deal to your grandfather. He was a good man, a good neighbor, and a good friend at a time when I felt very much alone in the world." Much to Catherine's relief, his shoulders relaxed. "Do you want to tell me what that was all about?"

Catherine's head shifted from side to side.

"Very well." He studied her a second longer and his expression softened. "You don't have to tell us anything if you don't want to, but I am going to let you know, whatever it is, whatever you need, you can count on every Farraday to stand at your side."

Most of the men in her life would have said their piece and walked away with little doubt that she would do as expected and follow their lead. Not so Sean Farraday. The man stood in front of her waiting for some response. All she could muster was a gentle nod. Had he told her to suck it up and get with the program, she might have known what to say, but she had no idea how to respond to such gentle strength. She had to wonder, what would her life have been like if she'd grown up in her grandfather's world or had a man like Sean Farraday for a father?

CHAPTER EIGHT

Maybe this was all a dream, or perhaps Connor had fallen down some crazy-ass rabbit hole like Alice in Wonderland. Two weeks ago he worked an oil rig, banked six figures a year, and was well on his way to cutting a deal for a place to start his own stable. Nowhere in that plan did having his heart stolen by a troubled little girl come into play.

"Do you like it?" Aunt Eileen asked the little girl.

Spoon in hand and lips covered in dribbles of apples, cream and chocolate sauce, Stacey blinked up at Eileen. Not a nod, or even a smile, but somehow every adult in the room knew the child had responded in the affirmative.

Pulling supper from the oven, Aunt Eileen set the large pan to the side and looked to Connor. "You better go see what happened to your father and brothers. We're just about ready to sit down to the table."

"May I help?" Catherine asked.

"I've got a pitcher of sweet tea in the fridge. If you'll get that, please."

Catherine pushed to her feet, and Connor turned to do as his Aunt had asked. In his father's office, D.J. sat at the computer. Finn and his father stood on either side of him leaning over his shoulders.

"Whoever you're chatting with, tell her goodnight. Supper's about to go on the table."

"It's not a her." D.J. looked up. "Not exactly."

The expression on his brother's face gave Connor pause.

D.J. pointed to the screen. "I'm sorry but there's bashful, there's teaching a child to be aware of strangers, and then there's something's very, damn wrong. I thought I should see what I could find out about the Hammonds."

"Always the policeman." Connor sucked in a breath and crossed the room. "Lots of kids are afraid of uniforms."

"Not like that," his father added.

Stacey's reaction *had* rattled him. "I thought you're not supposed to use police databases for personal interest?"

D.J. glared at Connor. "Google."

Sliding in between his two brothers, Connor scanned the information on the screens. Several different pieces on Catherine, her father's law firm, and a David P. Hammond Jr., the partner's son and Catherine's husband. Upon clicking further, a news article detailed the single driver crash that killed the man. Taking control of the mouse, Connor scrolled quickly. The mangled car wrapped around a tree gave little hope for the survival of any passenger. What was left of the driver side of the car appeared to be squeezed onto the passenger side. Scrolling some more he came across the photo that no doubt had everyone so engrossed in the data. A policeman holding a young child. Stacey. Her arms outstretched, her face warped with emotion, much like tonight, she appeared to be screaming bloody murder.

"Holy shit . . ." Connor muttered. "No wonder she freaked when she saw you. In the dimly-lit hall, tan pants, dark shirt, bright and shiny badge, similar build and coloring to that poor guy just trying to do his job."

"Says Stacey was alone in the car with her father." Biting down on his back teeth, D.J. swallowed hard. "No matter how you spin it, some days being a first responder really sucks."

A little further down a different article showed another picture of Stacey taken what must have been not long after the first photo. This time, held by an EMT and clutching the familiar stuffed dog, she was calmer. "Do you think Stacey has always been withdrawn, or do you think she's that way because of this?"

Muscles in D.J.'s jaw flexed before he moved his mouth to speak. "I'm no psychologist, but based on her response to my uniform, I'd say she has pediatric traumatic stress disorder—big time."

"I didn't know there was such a thing." Finn stepped back from the huddle.

"How long ago…?" Connor searched the screen for a date.

"Nearly two years," D.J. provided.

"Just like men." Aunt Eileen appeared in the doorway. "I swear it's genetic. Give y'all a cave and you don't come out til spring. Supper's on the table. Move it." She paused an extra moment scanning faces from left to right, raised one brow, dipped her chin, and clapped her hands. "Later. Supper's getting cold."

Supper wasn't the only thing chilled about now. Connor's blood was running cold.

• • •

"What are your plans after your grandfather's funeral," Aunt Eileen asked, taking a last bite of apple pie.

"Honestly, I'm not sure. I've only thought as far as getting through the service." Catherine wrapped her fingers around her empty tea mug.

For as long as Connor could remember, gathering around the dinner table was a sacred thing. Not until every single person had finished the last morsel on their plates could the group disband. Tonight he thought Aunt Eileen had been playing the Queen of England, toying with her food, keeping everyone in place.

"I need to go through the house," Catherine continued. "I suppose I was hoping I might find some of my mother's things."

Fork dangled in midair, Aunt Eileen's eyes lifted to meet Catherine's. "Honey, have you looked through the rooms upstairs?"

Catherine shook her head. "Not all of them. We're using the guest room off the kitchen. I've been focusing on Grandfather's office. Getting a handle on his business affairs. Every time I intend to look around more upstairs something pulled me away."

All eyes at the table turned to Catherine. Fortunately, she

didn't seem to notice the interest she'd drawn at the mention of Ralph's estate.

"Well, if you want to learn more about your mother, I suggest you explore the second floor. Last room on the left."

Catherine smiled. "Really?"

"Really." Aunt Eileen smiled back and pushed to her feet, collecting the empty pie plate. "It's a lovely night. Connor, why don't you show Catherine and Stacey around some of the nearby buildings? Stacey would probably enjoy seeing the foals."

"Oh, that won't be necessary." Catherine eased away from the table. "It's getting late."

"Nonsense," Aunt Eileen shook her head and looked to her brother-in-law.

"Eileen's right," Sean said. "There's been lots of changes 'round here since you last visited."

"I'm sure, but I'm not—"

"Better hurry," Aunt Eileen jerked a thumb over her shoulder. "Your daughter's got a jump start on you."

The screen door to the back porch was wide open and a flash of Stacey's brightly colored dress floated over the threshold seconds before the wood-framed door slammed shut with a loud slap.

"Stacey," Catherine called rushing across the expansive kitchen.

Knowing that Catherine was less than fond of ranch life, especially animals, Connor kicked his seat back, pausing at the sight of Finn's smug smile. "What's so funny?"

"'Just déjà vu, brother." Finn shook his head. "Just a little déjà vu."

Eileen pressed her lips tightly together, smacked her youngest nephew's shoulder, then turned to Connor. "You never mind. Go get those two."

"Yeah, brother," Finn's smile grew. "Go get 'em."

Halfway out the door, Connor heard his aunt smack Finn again and mutter, "Mind your manners."

***

"Stacey, sweetie, wait for Mommy." Why in heaven's name had Catherine dressed for dinner? Running after a five-year-old in heels was never fun. Doing it on uneven, ranch terrain was a sprained ankle in the waiting. For such a little kid, Stacey was already more than halfway to the barn.

"I'll get her." Connor whizzed past her just as Stacey turned the corner into the open barn door.

"Oh God. The animals." Catherine hiked up her skirt and rushed to catch up.

Ever since the car accident, her once smiling and bubbly child too easily withdrew into her own little world. In a near breathless panic from running and a spike of adrenaline, Catherine was all set to snatch her little girl from the perils of the big, bad ranch animals. Except there was no big, bad anything. Stacey had bypassed all the other stalls along the way and gone straight to Pharaoh.

At Stacey's side, Connor squatted, balancing on his boot heels, a big smile on his face. The upper half of the stall door was open and Pharaoh's head hung out and down. The horse's lips were moving and Catherine's first thought was that the horse was going to bite her too trusting daughter, but before Catherine could scream a shout of warning, her mind processed the full picture in front of her and she realized that Stacey was giggling. Not just making eye contact. Not simply lifting her lips in a smile, her newest thing since arriving in West Texas. Outright giggling. Cute, silly, little girl giggles. "Oh my God."

Connor sprang to his feet. "It's okay." He held up his hand to Catherine. "She's perfectly fine."

Any fool could see that. "I don't like horses," she mumbled. *They're dangerous.*

"I remember." Connor inched closer to her.

"You do?" She was sure none of the brothers remembered her. No one had said anything that gave the slightest indication to the contrary. Except for Mr. Farraday. And why did knowing any of them remembered her make her feel all calm and settled inside?

"I do." His head bobbed. "You never wanted to play with us kids."

"Yes, I did." She had. But the boys always wanted to do scary things like race ponies or tie ribbons on calf tails—and not fake calves like pin the tail on the donkey—the real ones that were squalling and running and kicking.

Connor shrugged. "I'm afraid I mostly remember seeing your back storming away and going home."

"I see." He was probably right. The last time she was here with her mother she couldn't have been much older than Stacey. And those horses looked so big. And the cattle. "Your father yelled at me."

"Really?" One dark eyebrow lifted high over very deep, crayon-blue eyes.

"You guys were doing something with the cows. I didn't have anything to do so Memah and my mother brought me here to play. I thought we could play hide and seek or Go Fish. Somehow I wound up not quite knowing where to go or what to do and the next thing I knew your father had scooped me up and scolded something I don't remember just as this big, black cow stomped on his foot. He tried not show it, but I could tell the animal hurt him."

Connor nodded. "Broke his foot. A several hundred-pound heifer will do that to you."

"Your father laughed it off and said he'd been kicked worse by his horse." She shook her head. She'd had nightmares with cows and horses running over her for months. "And my grandfather couldn't understand why I didn't like them."

"You didn't grow up on a ranch. I'm sure you were given a task that would have been easy for you."

"Help with the gate," she mumbled. But she'd gotten curious and walked closer.

Connor bobbed his head again. "Makes sense, but I'm guessing Dad kept an extra eye on you. Adam, too, probably."

"Maybe. I don't want . . ." Catherine pointed down the barn to the empty spot where her daughter no longer stood. "Oh my God, she must have opened the door." Heart lodged in her throat, the memories of almost being stomped on by an enormous ranch animal still vivid in her mind, Catherine's feet took off before her mind could process the horrors she'd find.

One foot forward, strong fingers manacled her arm. "Slow down. If you go charging off, you'll only spook the other animals."

"Or Pharaoh."

Connor shook his head. "No. If Stacey's in the stall with him, Pharaoh will know not to move. I trained him. He's very gentle." Still holding on to her arm, Connor guided her down the center of the barn to the next stall.

Inching forward, she didn't know if she'd find the strength to look. Not having heard her daughter scream in fear or pain was the only thing stopping her from racing to her baby.

One step ahead of her, Connor released his hold and coming to a stop, shifted to face the stall. A big smile sprouted on his face. "Told ya."

Peering into the enclosed space, her mouth actually fell open then snapped shut. "Should she be doing that?"

Connor hefted an indifferent shoulder. "Never met a good cow horse who didn't like to be brushed—"

"Cow horse?"

"Horse's bred and trained to work cattle. We can drop a rope to the ground to deal with a calf or cow and he won't move, that's called ground tie. If we're roping cattle and need the horse to give us slack or back up and add tension, a cow horse does exactly what's needed."

"Oh, but Stacey…"

"It's fine." He nodded, his attention on Stacey's every movement. "Make sure you don't step behind the horse. Okay?" he said softly.

The little girl barely bobbed her head. Topping out at only halfway up the huge horse's hindquarter, with two hands Stacey ran the brush from her highest reach down and then over slightly and back again.

The scene before Catherine was both horrifying and amazing. Everything in her screamed to carry her daughter out of here to safety, and yet, Stacey was nodding and responding. And the horse did look... cooperative. "He seems so docile."

"Pharaoh's a great horse. Good cow horses are worth their weight in gold. You should see Ginger. She's some of my foundation breeding stock."

"Breeding stock?"

He bobbed his head. "For the Capaill Stables. I'll be breeding and training the best quarter horses in the country."

She glanced back to make sure her daughter wasn't annoying the horse, then still unsure of how to deal with the sight before her, looked back to Connor. "Sounds ambitious."

"Not really. I've always loved horses. The Marines wasn't for me. I've been working for my own stables for years. Buying my own stock was the beginning. As a matter of fact—"

"But I thought you worked the ranch with your brothers."

"We all work the ranch from time to time, but Dad and Finn are the only ranchers. Adam, who you met last night, is a veterinarian. D.J. you know is the police chief. Brooks, who you haven't met yet, is a doctor. Ethan is a Marine helicopter pilot in theater so we don't see much of him. And you know Grace is in law school."

"Yes." Catherine glanced back at her daughter and was almost willing to swear the horse was falling asleep. Scanning the area, she didn't see anything that looked like horse care products. "Where did she find that?"

Pointing a finger at the next door over, Connor shook his head in a display of as much surprise as she'd felt. "She must have gotten the brush out of the tack room."

"Is she doing that right?"

He nodded. "Good enough."

"How does she know what to do?"

Those amazing, blue eyes twinkled. "Lady, your daughter

inherited the Brennan genes. Like it or not, Stacey is a natural horsewoman."

A soft sound reached her ears. "She's humming." Actually humming.

"She's happy," he said with the casualness only someone who didn't understand what that sound meant to a mother who had only heard nighttime screams since that horrible day.

"Yes. Yes, she is." And now what the hell was Catherine supposed to do about that?

CHAPTER NINE

The only way Connor and Catherine could get Stacey to leave the barn was to promise the little girl she could come back for a visit. For a second, Connor had seen an open door to discuss buying old man Brennan's property, but the conversation had veered off again and it hadn't felt right bringing it back around. The last thing he wanted was for Catherine to confuse his concern for Stacey with his desire for her grandfather's land.

Every time Connor looked at Stacey happily grinning at Pharaoh, his mind drifted to the horrible newspaper picture of her crying her heart out. If the thought gave him a sharp pain dead center of his chest, he couldn't fathom what Catherine had to feel. And from every overprotective reaction she had this evening to her daughter and ranch life, he couldn't think of a single reason why Catherine would want to stay in this part of the country. Why she wouldn't agree to sell the ranch. And why not to him once he secured the financing.

After the two had left, Aunt Eileen and Finn had called it an early night. Connor had gone back to the barn and taken Pharaoh a fresh apple and then given one to Ginger too. Normally on a quiet night, his thoughts would be full of plans for Capaill Stables. Homage to his Irish heritage. Coming up with the name itself had taken up too many conversations, batting ideas back and forth until one day, totally fed up with the horse talk, Finn said *just name the thing Horse Stables.* The corner of his aunt Eileen's lips had turned up. *Capall* she'd said. Then his dad shook his head and said, *not one, many. Capaill.* Just like that, his stables had found its name. From then on every quiet night had been spent mapping out the perfect layout for Capaill. When the idea had taken root to buy up the neighbor's property, plans came to mind on how to update and expand the barn, where to have the paddock, arena, hay storage, manure piles, anything and everything from pitchforks to fencing had been planned on nights like this.

Most people would have gotten started on the house. The few times he'd set foot inside, Connor had always felt like he'd walked into an episode of a seventies TV show and for now, that was fine with him. This deal was all about the horses. The Capaill Stables would have the best horse facilities in Texas.

His dream was so close he could feel the thrill of it all deep in his bones, and yet tonight, even in the stalls with his best four-footed friends, his mind had been cluttered not with trailers, tractors, and feed but with thoughts of Catherine. Every time shock and fear flashed in her eyes, he'd wanted to pull her into his arms and brush away the worry. Even when her eyes shone with wonder over her daughter and her new friend, he'd wanted to pull Catherine into his side and share the pleasure. Neither of which was a good idea.

The woman had been through enough the past couple of years. The last thing she needed was for someone like him to be prowling around her panties. And that had to be all it was. The caveman needs to protect and possess. There was no way he'd let himself consider it was anything more. The two of them were most definitely oil and water.

And he wasn't going to get anywhere out here spinning his wheels. The alarm clock rang early at the Farraday ranch. Even so, en route to the house, his gaze darted to his left toward the Brennan property. Not that he could see the house or any sign of life beyond the fence line, but he looked none the less and reminded himself, he and Catherine were nothing if not oil and water.

Taking a seat on the edge of the overstuffed sofa, Connor rested his forearms on his knees and blew out an exasperated sigh. "She was spooked by the cows."

"I know." In his favorite leather, high-back, easy chair, Sean

Farraday closed his book and removed his glasses. "She'd crawled into the pen just as Adam was about to open the gate and let the cows in."

"That was how you broke your foot."

His father shrugged. "Not the first time one of those critters got the best of us."

"Mm," Connor agreed. There had indeed been plenty of injuries through the years. Nothing life threatening, and all of them a lesson learned for next time.

The Farraday patriarch studied his son for so long Connor wondered what exactly the man was thinking. What did he want to say to him? It had been a very long time since the two had shared time alone together. Hell, in a house with seven children peace and quiet were precious commodities.

"She's nice, isn't she?" Sean's words invaded Connor's thoughts. "Catherine," he clarified.

"For a city girl." And she was a city girl. No country woman would show up to dinner in the outfit she had on. *Oil and water*. Not that there was anything wrong with dressing up on occasion, but ...

"You did good with the little girl, too," his father added.

Connor shrugged. "It was one hell of a surprise when Stacey wound up in my arms, but a soft word and a gentle touch works on a filly or a female equally well."

"That it does." Sean nodded.

"I hoped I would find these." Aunt Eileen came down the stairs, her arms fully loaded. "I'm not sure what size Stacey is, but one of these should be about right."

Sean Farraday frowned at his sister-in-law. "What are you doing up in the attic at this time of night?"

"It's only eight o'clock. That's not late for regular folk."

"Around here regular folk are ranch people, and eight o'clock is no time to be rummaging in the attic."

"I wanted Stacey to have something better than those sneakers to wear next time she comes to visit the horses. Bet she'd love to ride one of the ponies."

Aunt Eileen was partly right. Stacey definitely would enjoy being on one of the horses. Her mother, on the other hand, would probably see to it that Stacey viewed the animals from behind protective glass.

"Why don't you run these over in the morning after breakfast?" Eileen shoved the footwear at Connor.

By breakfast time he'll have put in hours of work. And smell like it too. "Maybe you should run them over."

Aunt Eileen didn't have to say a word. The stone-like expression on her face made it perfectly clear her suggestion was not a request.

"Or I can do it." Connor reached for the boots.

Instantly a bright smile bloomed on his aunt's face. "Good idea."

Actually, his aunt's idea probably wasn't a bad one. Dropping his sister Grace's old boots off for Stacey to use would be a good excuse to chat a bit about her plans for the property. Even if he didn't have the bank approval yet, he could at least ask about the ranch. The future home of the Capaill Stables, Connor Farraday Proprietor.

• • •

"Daddy, I don't want to go over this again." Catherine pinched the bridge of her nose and paced the large wood beamed living room.

"You don't hand off a prime case to a junior attorney to go off on some foolhardy trip to the middle of nowhere," her father rumbled.

"Grandfather's funeral is not foolhardy, and Connie is better than you think. She's hungry and smart—a lethal combination." Not that most of the men in that firm would notice. Especially not her father. The sole reason Catherine's gender had been overlooked by him and others at the firm was that William Everett Baxter didn't have a son. "Assign Ted Collins as second chair.

He'll hate it, but if it comes from you, he'll do it."

Her father blew out a deep sigh. "The client doesn't want Connie or Ted, he wants you."

Catherine stopped mid step.

"I need you back. ASAP. No more dilly-dallying in the wilderness."

Resuming her pacing, she looked out the expansive front window to the endless view of black velvet. No street lights. No neon signs. No honking horns. "Stacey seems to like it here."

"She'll like anywhere you take her, she's four."

"Five."

"Fine, five. Connie and Susan will continue the prep for depositions. I'm going to tell the client you will be here day after tomorrow—"

"The funeral is Sunday so the ranch families can attend."

"Catherine—"

"Sunday, Daddy."

"Fine. I'll tell the client you'll be ready to meet with him Monday—"

"I couldn't possibly—"

"Tuesday morning. That should be more than enough time to tie up whatever business you feel you need to do and come back where you belong. Where you've always belonged."

"Yes, Daddy."

"Goodnight. See you Tuesday."

"Tuesday." The call ended and Catherine did her best to ignore the sour churning in her stomach. She never should have answered the phone. What had she expected? Her father to give an understanding speech a la Sean Farraday? To ask her how she was handling the loss of an old man she'd barely begun to know? What she thought of the house she hadn't seen since childhood? The neighbors? The cowboy who had come rushing out to save Stacey from a wild beast. The same man who had tenderly soothed her distraught daughter in his arms. The one who followed his dreams. The one who...

Catherine stopped in her tracks. She couldn't be thinking of Connor Farraday. Not like this. Not now. He was a good-looking, nice guy. There were probably plenty of those in this part of the country. Hell, the Farraday house alone seemed to have an overabundant supply of handsome hunks. But she'd some of them already and D.J. and Adam weren't the ones who, in only two days, had made themselves at home in her thoughts.

She hadn't come here to meet a man. She didn't need to meet a man. She didn't want to meet a man. But every instinct she had told her Connor Farraday was no ordinary man.

• • •

"Stacey's mother isn't going to let her do anything more than wave at the barn animals from a distance and you know it." Sean Farraday stood. "Whatever it is you've got on your mind, forget about it. This is one newcomer who isn't going to be staying on."

"Have I said a word about that?" A few months ago, Eileen might have agreed with her late sister's husband, but after watching two city girls wander into town and fall in love with her nephews, she wasn't quite as skeptical as Sean.

"You don't have to." Sean walked up to his sister-in-law and standing beside her, rested one hand on her shoulder. It was a familiar gesture. One he'd used regularly over the last twenty plus years to show his support and concern. "I want all the boys happy too, but not every new woman who comes to town is meant to be a Farraday."

"I know that." And she did, but she'd seen Connor with women and children enough times to know the way he responded to Stacey was not a simple adult reaction. The way he stared at her mama when he thought no one was looking wasn't the way he looked at his sister or favorite aunt, either. There was something sparking between the two whether they knew it or not. All they needed was a little more time. "I wonder if Catherine plays poker?"

CHAPTER TEN

Normally Connor would never shower in the middle of the morning. Washing up always came at the end of the workday, but he just couldn't bring himself to go knocking on Catherine's door smelling like he'd just spent three hours with a herd of cattle. Even if he had indeed done just that.

Parking old Ruby in the front drive, he tossed his hat on the passenger seat and grabbed the bag loaded with his sister's childhood boots. By the time he'd come in for breakfast this morning Aunt Eileen had rounded up a few more pairs. He'd made a mental note that if he ever had children he would donate this sort of stuff rather than store a flea market in the attic for decades.

Stacey must have been near the front window because he'd not made it past the first step when the front door swung open and the little girl, still in footed pajamas and dangling the stuffed dog at her side by its floppy ear, stood staring at him. In only a few days he'd come to recognize the gleam in her eyes as happy or distraught and he was delighted to see a hint of pleasure at his appearance and equally disappointed not to have been gifted with a smile. Something he'd come to understand was indeed a gift.

"How's everyone this morning?" he asked, stopping in front of Stacey.

Rather than respond, she lifted the floppy-eared stuffed toy against her chest, turned her back to him and marched back inside. He supposed that was the closest thing to an invitation to come in he'd get. In the living room, she stood in front of the old twenty-five-inch TV half watching a cartoon program with dinosaurs and trains, and half watching him.

"Where's your mama?" Even though he'd asked, he hadn't really expected a response, so he was a bit surprised when her free arm shot up, pointing to the top of the stairs.

"Thank you, Miss Stacey." In a playful mood, he bowed at the waist like a British butler and was rewarded with a bright awareness in her gaze. He liked that. A lot. Gently mussing her hair with a pat, he took the stairs two at a time, calling out Catherine's name midway up. The last thing he needed was to startle the crap out of her and find himself full of buckshot. Not that a city girl would know what to do with one of Old Ralph's shotguns. Not hearing a word, he called out again, "Catherine? It's Connor from next door."

Carefully he inched his way down the hall, still carrying the bag of boots, a bit uneasy that she hadn't responded. Feeling more and more like a nervous cat burglar peeking into vacant rooms, he called her name again. Still no response, but this time he thought he heard sound coming from the end of the hall. Last door on the left, in the middle of the room, surrounded by books, books, and more books, Catherine sat staring intently at one in her lap.

"Excuse me." He rapped on the doorjamb before venturing in. "Looks interesting."

Catherine seemed to finally hear him and glanced up not nearly as surprised as she should have been to suddenly find herself accompanied by a man. "Oh, I didn't hear you." She set the book down and then, looking up again, waved her arm across the room. "They never changed it."

A quick glance told him he was in her mother's room. A wall of trophies from her barrel racing youth, high school pendants, mums from prom—those suckers seemed to get bigger every year decorated with more bling and ribbons than the year before. The dresser held a variety of girly looking perfumes and photographs of a woman who might have passed for Catherine's younger sister. "What are you looking at?"

"Mom wrote stories." She slid an envelope from a nearby box into the pages and closed the spiral notebook. "They're all over the place. I had no idea. Dad never said." Leaning to her left, she grabbed a bound book and sprang it open somewhere in the center.

"A yearbook. More kids than I would have thought for this small town."

"Lots of ranch families homeschool for the younger years, but by high school, the buses go all over the county picking kids up. Probably wasn't much different then."

Catherine handed it off to him. "She's all over that thing. If there was a club, she was in it. If there was a blue ribbon, she won it."

Flipping pages Connor noticed one more thing—if there was a horse involved she was on it. "She looks happy."

"Yeah, she does." Catherine brushed the remaining yearbooks and spiral notebooks and shoeboxes aside and pushed to her feet. "I found these things last night. The yearbooks were on the dresser but the notebooks and shoeboxes were in the closet. There's so much stuff in there."

"You planning on going through all of it?" He closed the yearbook.

"I don't know. I have to be back in Chicago on Tuesday." Tired eyes scanned the remnants of a life long gone. "I don't know how much I can get done by then, but I'm realizing just how daunting sorting through generations of family history is going to be."

That did not sound good for Connor. Not if he wanted to start work on the barn and have it in suitable shape before winter kicked in. "Didn't Aunt Eileen and some of the ladies from the social club offer to help?"

"They did." She nodded. "And I was going to take them up on it, but now, now I think I want to go through it all myself. I don't want to miss anything."

Connor took another look around. The closet was indeed packed with years of clutter, but how hard could sorting through old clothes and shoes and miscellaneous teenage sundries take?

"And you should see the attic. I don't know that the Brennans have thrown anything out since the birth of Christ."

Asked and answered. Sorting through years of family history

was going to take longer than from now til Tuesday which meant even if the bank came through for him quickly, his chances of getting the land anytime soon were next to nil. Damn. A tiny pump jackhammered at his temple. That bank letter might be the only chance he'd have to set a light under her. He glanced around at the mounds of her mother's belongings. *Or not.*

"What do you have in the bag?" Catherine lifted her chin in the direction of his right arm.

"Oh. Aunt Eileen sent these over." He handed over the boots. "They were my sister Grace's. She outgrew most of them long before she ever wore out a pair."

Catherine pulled out a tiny cowboy boot, turning it left than right.

"They're for Stacey," he added before his brain could filter the stupidity of the statement.

"I see. I think it's a safe bet Stacey will be pleased." She smiled at him and then returned her attention to the remaining contents.

It was a nice smile. A very nice smile. One he wouldn't mind seeing again.

"There's an entire hall closet filled with clothes," she said, replacing a boot in the bag and turning toward the door. "I'm thinking by the length of the pants they belong to my mother. Her mom is much shorter than her in the photos I've found."

Connor looked at several family photos side by side. Mrs. Brennan was indeed a petite thing. From what he remembered of her, until she got sick, she was strong as an ox and anyone who only took in her size learned fast not to underestimate her again. "The word fireball comes to mind."

A slow, lazy grin pulled at one side of Catherine's mouth. "I like that. I've heard that word used a time or two to describe me in the courtroom. I wouldn't mind thinking I inherited that from my grandmother."

"You should be proud. Everyone loved her."

"I am." Catherine took a step forward. "Have you had

breakfast yet?"

Yep. A rancher's breakfast. The kind that would stick to his ribs and keep him energized for hours of hard labor. "Just a bite."

"Good. I'm not much of a cook, but I've been told I make a mean omelet. Join us?"

"Thank you, I think I will." No one ever died from eating two breakfasts. At least not that he knew of.

● ● ●

"Everything is set for Sunday." Catherine nodded to the table of women in her kitchen. "I must say, deciding on some of the details has been more challenging than I'd expected."

"Like what?" Aunt Eileen leaned forward.

"Well, someone has to give a eulogy. I didn't know if Grandfather had any close friends." Catherine paused for a breath in case the women had a suggestion she was unaware of. "I've been looking through things around the house, but don't see any sign of a close friend from recent years."

"He was close to Clinton Farley," Sally May said. "But he passed a good ten years ago."

"And sometimes he'd go into town and chew the fat with Ned at the service station." Ruth Ann chimed in. "But come to think of it, didn't they have a falling out over something?" Two sets of eyes glared at Ruth Ann. "Okay, maybe Ned isn't the best idea."

"I had a feeling, so I thought perhaps I could convince Mr. Farraday to give the eulogy. They've been neighbors a long time and—"

"And that's a wonderful idea. Sean will be happy to. Your grandfather was a good and respected man who simply kept to himself these last few years."

"Oh good." There was no way Catherine could express what a relief it was to have that taken care of. "Next, the pastor suggested Grandpa's friends would want to attend the graveside service?"

Three heads bobbed. "Yes, sirree. That's the way it's done

around here."

"The pastor also suggested refreshments at the church after the services. If Grandfather doesn't have many friends left, maybe we can skip—"

This time, three heads shook in unison with parade precision.

"I don't want to tell you how to plan your grandfather's services." Eileen reached over and covered Catherine's fisted hands with her own. "Ralph may have been a solitary old man, but he had friends. Don't you think for one minute he wasn't loved by every neighbor and every town person he crossed paths with. His funeral is going to bring a full house."

"Oh." That wasn't exactly what she'd expected to hear. Her gaze shifted immediately around the old country kitchen.

"And don't you worry about the food either," Sally May said.

"That's right," Ruth Ann added. "The Tuckers Bluff Ladies Afternoon Social Club will take care of that. Is there anything else you need from us?"

"Well." She looked over at Stacey on the living room floor, folded over the coffee table, using every single color crayon in the huge box that Eileen had brought over. Catherine could see hours of entertainment in store for her little girl. "I suppose I do need to sort through clothes. See if anything can be useful to anyone."

"You bet." Sally May was the first to her feet. "There's lots of families in this county who need a helping hand."

"And lots more with a way with needle and thread to make secondhand look store-bought new." Ruth Ann moved beside her friend. "You bring the boxes?"

Sally May grinned from ear to ear at Catherine. "Just in case."

"I may have said something." Eileen lightly placed her hand on Catherine's arm. "We're ready to work if you want the help."

Catherine looked at all the women in the room ready to roll up their sleeves at her okay. The antithesis of the corporate legal world where backstabbing was common place and emotional Kevlar was the dress of the day. What an interesting place her mother had left behind. "Thank you, ladies. I'd like that."

CHAPTER ELEVEN

"What in the world?" Connor wiped his boots at the back door and hung his hat on the nearby hook. Finding Stacey at the kitchen table was not what he'd expected.

Immersed in her work, the little girl didn't look up.

Connor scanned the kitchen and glanced down the hall. No sign of anyone. Beside the kitchen sink a large platter of oatmeal raisin cookies rested next to a huge pitcher of lemonade. He didn't need to have a PI license to know what his aunt had been doing this afternoon. Snatching a couple of cookies from the plate, he moved over to stand beside Stacey. "That's really good."

With an open box of crayons and stacks of blank paper nearby, she worked on a darn impressive picture of the Appaloosa Adam usually rode when on the ranch. He glanced at some of the other pictures she'd drawn. All horses. Some with grass at their feet. Some with a house in the background. From underneath one of the pictures she pulled out a sheet of paper and handed it to him. Pharaoh.

"I think this is my favorite," he smiled down at her.

"Oh good. You're back early." Aunt Eileen dropped a basketful of clothing on the table. "I found some more of Grace's things."

"Where's Catherine?" Connor asked.

"She's gone into town with Sally May and Ruth Ann. By lunchtime, we'd sorted through all of Ralph and Marjorie's clothes in the master bedroom and even made it through the downstairs linen closet. Anything that didn't look like a family heirloom went into the donation box."

Connor nodded and waited.

"There were enough boxes to just fit in the back of Sally May's Suburban. We all figured it would be a good thing to take the load into town and dole out the treasures. Figured little Stacey here would have more fun coloring and watching TV than traipsing around town with a bunch of old ladies."

"Mm." Now things were starting to make sense. "And you volunteered to bake cookies with Stacey."

"Well, it seemed like a good idea once we got here." His aunt smiled. "Sweetie," Eileen turned to the little girl, "I think it's time to feed the babies again. You ready?"

Stacey bobbed her head, put the crayon back in the box, and slid off the chair. That's when Connor noticed she was wearing a pair of the boots he'd brought over as well as a pair of jeans.

"Her mother dressed her in jeans?"

Aunt Eileen shrugged. "I found a few pairs." She waved at an open box on the other side of the kitchen stacked on top of a few more boxes. "I also found some of her riding gear."

"Riding gear?"

"There's a pair of butter-soft chaps that should be just about—"

"Chaps? What could she possibly need chaps for?"

"So the calves don't kick her."

This wasn't going well. Connor rubbed the back of his tired neck. "She's not going to be near any calves."

"Of course she is. How else will she learn to tie the tails for next month's Ranchathon?"

"They're going home after the funeral. And even if they weren't leaving right away, Stacey has never been around ranch animals. She wouldn't know what to do with a calf or a mutton. And even if she did, there is no way on this green earth her mother is going to let her participate in the ranch games with the other kids."

"You never know." His aunt shrugged casually.

Implied indifference from his aunt was never a good thing. "Aunt Eileen."

"Oh, don't be such a sour puss. Stacey's been waiting for you or Finn to get done with your chores so she can see the foals. Maybe brush down some of the smaller animals. Learn a thing or two about feeding."

"Shall I teach her the pros and cons of fall calving in our spare time?"

Aunt Eileen smacked him on the arm. "Don't get sassy with me young man."

Bright, blue eyes stared up at him. Stacey had watched the conversation with invested intensity. He could see how badly she wanted to do whatever his aunt had said. And though he might pay the price when her mother found out, there was no way in hell he was going to disappoint her. Sticking his hand out, he blew out a breath. "Ready to go?"

Stacey's tiny hand slid into his. Folding his large hands around hers, he worried they might be too rough against her soft skin, but before he could reconsider and pull back, she was practically dragging him out the door. Grabbing his hat as they crossed the threshold, he shook his head. Her mother was going to kill him.

On a ranch as big as the Farradays there was one thing to be sure of. With every season of new life, there would be some loss. Which meant at any given time there would be a calf or foal without their mama. Inside the barn, he squatted down to be at eye-level with his new charge. "There are lots of rules on a ranch."

To his surprise, Stacey nodded. Maybe his aunt was onto something.

"For now, you stay by me and do exactly as I say."

This time, she blinked but he recognized the affirmation in her eyes.

"Never walk behind any of the animals." He waited and when she realized he wasn't going to say anything more without some reaction from her, she nodded. His heart did a quick two-step. "Never get close enough to touch an animal without a grown up at your side."

She nodded again.

"We're going to give Pharaoh and some of the other horses a little snack. Then we'll check on the foals. Okay?"

This time, she only blinked. He wished he knew what constituted being worthy of a nod and what only warranted a blink, but two out of four were pretty good odds. Grabbing a handful of treats from the tack room, he put them into his pocket and took Stacey to Pharaoh's stall first. Immediately the big animal dropped his head to meet her. She looked up at Connor in a silent request to approach the horse, but before Connor could respond, Pharaoh had inched forward and nudged her shoulder with his nose.

A move that could have frightened most children unfamiliar with animals had Stacey giggling. Immediately her arms swung as far as they could reach around the horse's neck.

"Easy there." Connor waited a second before pulling her back and placing her palm flat against his neck. "Every horse appreciates a good rub along here."

As though stroking a stray house pet, Stacey passed her hand along Pharaoh's side over and over.

"Okay now." Connor squatted beside her. "Hold your hand out flat."

Stacey quickly opened her hand. Connor deposited the treat, and bless Pharaoh for being a patient fellow, he waited while Connor continued to explain. "You're going to place your hand under his nose so he can eat the snack. His lips may tickle your palm, but you keep your hand in place till he's done. Okay?"

Eyes twinkling, she nodded.

Connor sucked in a deep breath and watched the little girl do exactly as she had been told, her cheeks pulling back into a broad smile as the horse's lips covered and retrieved the hard apple-flavored nugget. When the horse was done, without instruction, Stacey returned to stroking his neck, her smile intact. The kid was definitely a natural.

Moving down the stalls, Stacey had made friends with Brooks' Appaloosa when Finn rode into the barn, his face covered with surprise. Dismounting, Finn ran his hand between the horse's front legs.

"He need cooling down?" Connor asked.

Finn shook his head. "Walked him in. You've already got Pharaoh put away?"

"Yeah, I finished up with the west pasture early."

By the spigot, Finn grabbed a bucket and filled it with water. "I see you had a helper."

Connor shook his head. "We've just been visiting."

From the moment Finn had ridden in, Stacey had watched him intently. Her gaze followed the way he'd slipped his feet out of the stirrups and climbed off the horse, to what he'd done with the reins and how he'd checked if Ace had cooled off enough before getting him a drink.

"Aunt Eileen made cookies," Connor said.

Finns eyes widened with interest. "Chocolate chip?"

"Oatmeal raisin."

"That'll work." Finn smiled.

Connor looked at Stacey again and ran calculations through his head at lightning speed. How old had all the Farraday children been when they'd learned to care for a horse, what had his aunt promised the little girl, and how much time would he need to outrun Catherine when she found out what he was about to do. "Why don't you go on inside, we'll put Ace away."

One eyebrow shooting up higher than the other, Finn glanced at Stacey then back to his brother. "You sure?"

Connor nodded and Finn shrugged, patted his horse on the neck, whispered in his ear to behave, and turned on his boot heel for the house.

Clapping his hands together, Connor turned to Stacey. "Ready to take care of Finn's horse?"

For venturing into the dangerous territory of potentially really pissing off the woman he wanted to buy the stable land from, Connor was rewarded with a smile *and* a nod. Things were looking up.

"First we need to give him some water." Connor intentionally filled the bucket only half full, hoping it was light enough for Stacey to handle. "Here you go."

She grabbed the handle and, carrying it with more ease than he would have expected, she held the water in front of the horse and shot Connor another grin as Ace slurped up the contents.

"When we get to the stall we'll give him some more water if he wants." Stacey's gaze narrowed on the bucket and Connor knew she had a question and waited foolishly hoping she'd simply ask it. "If you give him too much water right away he'll get colic, a really painful upset gut."

The little girl's eyes cleared with understanding. With Stacey at his side, they undid the tack, removed the saddle, and even though Connor carried the brunt of the weight, Stacey held on with both hands, her brow furrowed with concentration. The kid had grit.

For the next ten minutes or so, he and Stacey brushed the animal using the same soothing strokes she'd used the other night on Pharaoh. "This," he explained, "is to bring up all the dust and dirt and sweat that gets caught up in his hair while working."

Stacey didn't nod or answer, she didn't break her concentration to look at Connor, but he knew, as with everything else they'd done, she was processing every word and action.

Next, Connor used the stiff brush to flick off any loose dirt and then, with the pride of a trainer on race day, watched Stacey use the soft brush on Ace's face and feet. If he didn't know better he'd have sworn she'd been around horses all her life. While he went from foot to foot, cleaning out the hooves and removing any rocks, Stacey leaned against him.

Having led the horse into his stall, Connor handed Stacey an apple half he'd grabbed from the tack room. "Why don't you give him this as a reward for being such a cooperative boy?"

Intentionally, he didn't say anything, curious to see what Stacey would remember from before, confident that even if she'd done something differently Ace wouldn't pose a threat. But he needn't have worried. Opening her palm, with the apple centered, she held her hand under the massive animal's muzzle and waited patiently as he nibbled then gobbled the fruit. Since Ace wasn't quite as enamored with Stacey as Pharaoh and hadn't dropped his head for her, she simply reached up and rubbed the side of his jaw.

"I still have to clean his tack. You ready to go back inside with Aunt Eileen?"

The hint of a smile that had graced her face slipped. For a split second he thought that maybe Ace had moved and somehow hurt her, but then it hit Connor.

"Do you want to help me?" he asked.

She gave a slight bob of her head.

"All right then." He smiled at her and held out his hand. "Saddle cleaning lesson 101 coming up."

CHAPTER TWELVE

"It was nice of you to give me a lift back to the house." Catherine had spent the better part of the afternoon accompanying Ruth Ann to various homes in the outlying area. Most of the items she'd brought in had been left with the pastor, but he'd given them a list of some folks who had expressed a need for assistance. Adding some of her donations to bundles already waiting, Catherine and Ruth Ann went off in one direction and Sally May and another church lady in the other.

It was Catherine's good luck to have crossed paths with D.J., who was heading out to the ranch.

"Ruth Ann doesn't live far from the ranch by West Texas standards, but I was heading that way anyhow."

"You spend a lot of time at the ranch?"

"Some days more than others." D.J. tapped his finger on the edge of the steering wheel.

Catherine didn't know this Farraday brother well, but she'd been reading witnesses and jurors long enough to recognize a man with something unpleasant on his mind. "Tough day?"

"You could say that." His finger continued to tap on the wheel.

Catherine was pretty sure he didn't realize what he was doing. His gaze focused on the emptiness of the road stretching out in front of them. Whatever was going on in that Farraday mind was none of her business, but she took a shot at it anyhow. "Business or personal?"

D.J. slanted her a glance. "In a town this size, business is almost always personal."

"The place isn't that small." Driving around today she'd realized Tuckers Bluff and the outlying homes technically in the town's limits were as big as many suburbs of Chicago, just a little more space spread out in between.

"Getting bigger every day."

"Why is that?"

"Oil keeps us busy and the business and people who come with it."

"But we're pretty far from the big cities." At least it felt that way when she was driving here from Dallas.

"We are. When I was young every kid in town dreamed of escaping the redneck lifestyle."

"Even you?"

"Even me. And like me, folks are coming back. Finding a way to make life and family work in the less hectic pace."

"Dorothy and Oz. There's no place like home."

D.J. nodded. "Something like that."

"So who has you all twisted? No need to mention names, not that I'd know who they are anyway."

"It's a matter of public record. I had to take a call today. Domestic abuse."

Catherine waited.

"I went to school with the guy. Salt of the earth. And now..."

"Now there's trouble in paradise."

D.J.'s head nodded up and down. "He's cooling off in jail."

Something told her locking up his high school buddy wasn't all that was bothering him. "Surely this isn't the first time you've had to arrest someone you knew?"

He shook his head. "I'll figure it out."

"I'm sure you will." And she was. It was obvious he cared about the people in his town. And that concern was what made the best cops. Glancing out the side window, her mind wandered back to Stacey and all that had happened in just a few days. "I hope my daughter wasn't too much for your aunt."

"That'll be the day." D.J. huffed with amusement.

She was pleased to see this Farraday brother smile. "Why is that?"

"There isn't a kid in this county my aunt can't handle, and Stacey leans heavily on the nice kid scale. There won't be a problem. I predict Aunt Eileen is either baking up a storm or dressing up for a tea party."

"She did lots of tea parties with you boys, did she?" Catherine swallowed a smile.

"Hardly." D.J. shook his head again, still smiling. "I suppose she went a bit overboard with Grace to offset all the testosterone running around the house."

"So what you're telling me is expect her to spoil my girl?"

His chin dipped. "Something like that."

Talk about noncommittal. She was starting to think "something like that" was on his top ten hit parade of phrases. And she hoped deep down inside that maybe Aunt Eileen could reach Stacey in a way no one else had. Except maybe for Connor's horse. Or that strange dog.

● ● ●

"Don't you look pretty as a picture." Aunt Eileen surveyed Stacey in one of the ruffled dresses she'd made for Grace when she'd thought she wanted to take square dancing lessons. That fad had lasted all of about an hour after the dress was finished. Connor remembered the incident clearly. Along with the forgotten piano lessons and ballet classes. The only thing that stuck was horses. Probably genetic.

Stacey twirled, lifting the skirt in a wide circle and then sidled up beside Connor's aunt at the kitchen sink. "You ever peel potatoes?"

Stacey's head shifted a fraction left then right. Not a full-fledged shake, but enough, and Connor wondered if it was merely a case of losing her bashfulness or if spending time with the animals was really helping. Or maybe he was overthinking a problem that was none of his business.

Aunt Eileen handed over a potato, pulled a chair up to the

sink and, setting Stacey on top of it, stood behind the eager little girl, arms around her, like a puppeteer with her marionette to show how to maneuver the small kitchen gadget.

"Anybody home?" D.J.'s voice came from the front of the house.

Since when did any of the brothers announce themselves? The Farraday house might as well have had a revolving door for friends and family who always, without fail, wound up in the kitchen. Connor was just about to open his mouth and shout to his brother when Catherine appeared.

"I caught a ride with the police chief." Catherine flashed an impish grin.

A few steps behind her, D.J. came into view, sans a badge or belt that usually holstered his gun, his uniform shirt untucked and mostly unbuttoned. In all the times Connor had seen his brother in uniform, as a Marine, a Dallas cop, or Tucker Bluff police chief, never had D.J. looked so…sloppy. It made Connor smile. None of the Farraday men might know much about little girls, but they cared enough to break any rule rather than frighten one again.

The moment Aunt Eileen laid eyes on D.J., the big smile on her face fell. Connor took a second look. Other than the untucked shirt, nothing out of the ordinary jumped at him. D.J. wore the same stone-faced expression he always did. Then again, growing up, the kids often wondered if Aunt Eileen had inherited some Irish fairy power and could read minds. Lord knew if ever they tried to skirt the truth she called them on it. And if she didn't call them on it, she taught them a lesson later.

"Where's Dad and Finn?"

"One of the wranglers noticed a calf stuck in the pond. Sean and Finn left a few minutes ago."

Focused on her potato, Stacey didn't even turn around to acknowledge her mother, not even when Catherine sidled up beside her and gave her a peck on the top of her head.

"Did you have a good day, baby?" Catherine asked.

Stacey bobbed her head once without looking up and

Catherine's eyes grew round as the full moon outside, then her head whipped in Aunt Eileen's direction, her gaze flying from the older woman to Connor and back to her daughter.

So maybe it was more than just a case of Stacey being bashful around strangers. And maybe Aunt Eileen had been dead right about the horses.

"Supper's almost ready, have you eaten yet?" his aunt asked Catherine.

The still stunned mother shook her head but kept her gaze on her daughter.

"Good. Then you'll stay."

Catherine nodded, slowly stepped away from Stacey, and looked up at Eileen. "Anything I can help with?"

"Nope. Stacey and I have everything under control. Why don't you and the boys go sit a spell. I've got some blueberry lemonade I'll bring in."

Connor set his hand along the small of Catherine's back and nudged her into the other room, her gaze occasionally drifting over her shoulder to her daughter happily peeling an enormous stack of potatoes.

By the time everyone had taken a seat, Aunt Eileen entered the room with a tray of glasses. "Here we are." She set the tray on the handcrafted square coffee table in the middle of the room then, taking a quick peek at Stacey, looked to D.J. "What happened?"

D.J. pinched the bridge of his nose. "Jake Thomas went for Charlotte's throat in the middle of the Silver Spurs."

Aunt Eileen's slender fingers lifted to cover her surprise. "Is she okay?"

D.J. nodded. "Half the town sprang into action. He's sitting in my jail as we speak."

"And Charlotte?"

"I left her with Brooks. She seems more shaken up than anything. Will probably have some bruising. The thing is, it took Adam, Burt, and Frank to pull Jake off of her. From eyewitness reports, if I didn't know Jake, I'd swear the guy they described was high on some heavy duty drugs."

Connor knew what his brother was referring to. Some drugs made men, and women, crazy strong. On leave in South Florida, he'd seen a woman high on Flakka kick out the rear window of a squad car. Crazy.

"Brooks drew a blood sample. Sent it off for testing. I'll know in a day or two. But I can't believe it."

"You know, at the café yesterday I heard that it's not just his wife he's angry at."

D.J. dropped his hand to his side and faced his aunt. "What did you hear?"

"Burt Larson said he'd tore into Jim Brady. And Mrs. Peabody said something happened with Tess Rankin. What can make a man change like that?"

"Well, at least this time I can hold Jake in custody without needing Charlotte to press charges, but…"

No one needed to finish D.J.'s sentence. Locking Jake up might stop the abuse for now, but it wouldn't fix a broken family. Especially if what Connor had heard from his brothers was true and Charlotte Thomas continued to defend her husband.

"Maybe I can be of some help." Catherine set her lemonade on a side table. "I've done some pro-bono work for a shelter in Chicago. If anyone thinks it would do any good, I'd be glad to talk to the wife."

"That's very kind of you, but I'm not sure it will do much good at this point." D.J. shifted forward. "I've been trying to talk some sense into her but she's stubborn. The other officers and I have been doing extra patrols on the Thomas' street. Stopping into the feed store more often. Even Adam has tried to invite Jake out, talk some sense into him, convince him to get some help—"

"And no one is getting anywhere," Catherine added. "It's a damn sorry mess."

"I'd better get back to my helper in the kitchen." Eileen stepped away and paused. "Twenty-five years in this town and we've never had this happen before. I don't know what to do." Not expecting an answer, she plastered on a smile for Stacey and hurried back to the kitchen and her impromptu cooking lesson.

CHAPTER THIRTEEN

"It was really sweet of you to carry her in like this," Catherine whispered as she held the door open for Connor.

Spending the day at the Farraday's had worn Stacey out. When time to leave had finally rolled around, Stacey had ignored her mother until Catherine promised that she could visit again tomorrow. Once they'd all climbed into Connor's old truck, he'd barely turned the ignition on when exhaustion won out and Stacey nodded off to sleep.

"No problem. Which way?" Connor paused at the door and shifted Stacey onto his shoulder with the practiced ease of a loving father. Immediately she'd curled into him, her fingers searching and settling against his neck.

The sight stole Catherine's breath. "We're sleeping in here." Leading the way to the downstairs guest room off the kitchen, Catherine glanced over her shoulder memorizing the image of her daughter safely tucked into Connor's shoulder. Whipping the sheets back on the large bed she and Stacey shared, she eased away making room for Connor to set the girl down. The second her head touched the pillow, she rolled onto her side and curled into the mattress. Catherine removed her socks and shoes under Connor's watchful eye and avoided the risk of waking up Stacey with any attempt at putting on her pajamas.

Softly, Catherine closed the door behind them and waved Connor into the main room. "I hope she sleeps through the night again."

"Doesn't like a strange bed?" Connor paused beside her.

"Maybe, but she's had trouble with nightmares since her father died. They've lessened with time. Used to be every night.

Sometimes twice a night. Now it's dwindled to a couple of times a week. She'd slept through the night before we left Chicago and hasn't woken up since we arrived here. If she sleeps through the night, it may be her longest streak of good night sleeps yet."

"I'm sorry to hear that." His gaze drifted toward the closed door of Stacey's room. "She's such a sweet kid."

"She used to be really happy. I won't kid you. My husband and I worked insane hours. I guess you could say we were two workaholic peas in a pod. Eighty-hours was a short work week for us. Most of Stacey's waking hours were spent with a nanny. There were days when we didn't see her at all, but she *was* a happy girl."

Connor turned his attention back to Catherine, but to her surprise, his gaze didn't hold judgment or contempt. More like curiosity, or perhaps understanding.

"I'm sorry, I didn't mean to dump on you." Working crazy hours left little time for developing friendships, and her father certainly didn't want to hear anything that remotely sounded like a complaint. All her life she'd been raised to have a thick skin and take it like a man. And she had. Except where it came to Stacey. "I've said too much."

"No. I…I'd like to hear more."

Catherine nodded. She wanted to share her little girl with someone besides a therapist making vain and empty promises. "Let's take a seat on the back porch, that way I can hear if she wakes up."

A step behind, Connor followed her out to the porch, waited for her to take a seat on the old glider and leaning against the rail, crossed his ankles. "What happened?"

Catherine steeled her spine and thought back to life two years ago. "She loved people. And she adored her father. David wasn't really very playful. Neither one of us was the kind of parent to play games or roughhouse. A walk in the park was just that—a walk. The few hours we could steal as a family were spent at a museum or gallery, rather than a park or playground. But mostly quality time meant Stacey on David's lap while he read a Louis L'amour novel out loud or I read her Dickens."

"You read Dickens to a toddler?" The surprise in his eyes made Catherine smile.

"Well, the children's illustrated version."

Connor smiled and tipped his head in a vague gesture that showed neither assent nor disagreement and then his smile grew. "Was there a children's illustrated version of Louis L'amour?"

"Nope." She took in a calming breath to steady the flutters that seemed to develop whenever he flashed that lazy smile at her. "The real thing. Just like her father, she loved it."

"Daddy's little girl," Connor said lightly.

Catherine nodded. "That evening I was supposed to pick up Stacey at a special daycare program while our regular nanny was on vacation. I got wrapped up in work and, well, time got away from me." Her toe pushed hard on the floor and set her rocking. "David had gone home early with a touch of flu. He was closer to Stacey than I was, so he picked her up."

"And then the accident happened?"

Hugging her arms, she nodded. "David was killed instantly. Stacey unbuckled her car seat and the first officer on the site found her crawling on her father, crying for him to wake up. He had to break the glass to get her out. She still has a little scar right here." Catherine pointed to the edge of her temple. "She hasn't said a word since."

Connor blinked long and hard. "I'm sorry. I don't know what to say."

"There's nothing to say. It happened. We're dealing with it."

"Are you?"

Two words had her feet flattening on the wooden porch and stopping the glider's motion. She'd tried a few therapists, psychiatrists, even herbologists. None of it had helped. And now it looked like she was going to try fresh air and country living. "I've lost too many people in my life. I can't let anything happen to Stacey. She's all I have left."

Nodding, Connor bobbed his head. "What about your father?"

"Dad eats and breathes the law. Maybe he was different when my mother was alive." She shrugged. "I wasn't much older than Stacey when my mother got sick and died. I've never known Dad to be any different."

"No other grandparents?"

"Dad's parents traveled a lot. When they're not, home is an old brownstone in Philadelphia. As for my mom's parents, Dad never mentioned them again. I guess I just thought they died with Mom."

Connor bobbed his head and looked off into the distance and back. "I'm sorry. The Brennans were nice people. You would have liked them."

"I know. At least I got a little while with my grandfather thanks to modern technology."

"There is that." He smiled.

"What about you?" Catherine leaned forward. She'd had enough of a walk down her own memory lane. "You mentioned wanting to breed horses?"

Connor bobbed his head. "Yeah. As a kid, when everyone else was gathering cattle or separating calves or mending fence lines, I liked to sneak off and watch the wild mustangs." He smiled. More of a sly grin that made her want to smile too. "I could watch them for hours. Got pretty close to them a time or two. Some days it was almost as if I could read their minds." He shrugged. "Turns out horses like me, too."

On her feet, she crossed the small porch and leaned against the rail beside him. "What do you mean?"

"I have a knack. If there's a troubled horse. A difficult horse, folks would bring him to me. I'd work him through it."

"You mean like a horse whisperer?"

Connor's smile burst into a rumbling laugh. "Not really. It's just a matter of understanding equine mentality. Earning the horse's trust. Too many people want to break the will of these majestic animals." He shook his head and sighed.

Leaning back, Catherine studied the strength of his gaze. Eyes are the windows to the soul. In Connor's she could see a steel will and the heart of a lion. Her ability to read people all these years had served her well. "You'll get what you want."

Only inches apart, his gaze latched onto hers. Heat and hunger stared back at her. Everything around her faded into the distance. The air between them sparked with electricity. He sucked in a deep breath, closed his eyes and then opening them slowly, lifted his finger to her cheek, blew out that long awaited breath, and whispered, "Will I?"

Without any thought, her chin dipped, nodding agreement. The question was would she get what she wanted too.

• • •

Insanity had taken over. That was the only explanation for why all reason had vanished and the only thing that Connor felt or thought was the undeniable need to taste this woman. His fingertips burned and his heart slammed against his ribs. This was so not a good thing to do. Not smart. Kissing her could only lead to trouble. And he so didn't care.

Sliding his free hand around her waist, with a gentle nudge, she toppled fully into his arms. Soft breasts pressed against his hard chest. What little blood was left in his veins rushed south of his belt buckle. And still, he didn't care.

A startled breath caught in her throat, the sound heightening his senses. Slowly, in complete contrast to the urgency racing inside him, his lips met hers. Soft, pliable, and perfect. Fingers digging into his chest eased away and with another purring sound that had his jeans feeling tight and uncomfortable, her arms eased around his neck pulling him impossibly closer.

Had he ever wanted any woman as much as he wanted Catherine? A simple kiss felt like everything he could ever need and at the same time not enough. He wanted so much more, and yet if this was all he'd ever had he would settle for it for the rest of his life.

Rest of his life? The words rattled around in what was left of his brain. Need and want clawed and scratched their way to the surface. The hand around her waist slid lower, resting on the curve of her back. The simple weight of it shifted her hips, rubbing against him, shooting darts of anticipation in every direction. He could happily sink into her every day of his life, starting tonight.

An obnoxious glimmer of chivalry rapped at the doors of his mind. Her daughter at this very moment slept only yards away. Catherine had to be reeling in the emotional losses of her husband, her grandfather, and in some ways her daughter. His father's words slapped all thoughts aside with the clarity of a bullhorn: *There are rules. Never take advantage of a lady whose been drinking, been crying, or been suffering. Never.*

Using every ounce of sheer will he possessed, Connor pulled away, took a half step in retreat and let his forehead rest against Catherine's. Breathing way heavier than he should have been, and still desperately wanting to lose himself inside her, he scrambled for words. Not any words. The right words. "I'm sorry," was all that came out. Too bad he didn't have a clue what he was sorry for.

"I'm not." She lifted her head, and stepping back until she rested against the porch rail, she kept her gaze on him. "Tell me more."

"More?" His mind was not firing on all pistons. At this moment most of the blood in his body had abandoned his brain and settled south of his belt buckle.

"About your dream. Are you going to expand the ranch?"

Right now the last thing he wanted to do was talk, but maybe now was as good a time as any. "I want my own place. My own stable."

"Your own space."

"You make is sound like I'm running away from home."

She chuckled and the soft rumble made him laugh too. "Sorry. So you want your own ranch. When do you want this to happen?"

"Now."

"Now?"

"I'm just waiting for some paperwork from the bank."

"Approval?" she asked.

He bobbed his head. "It's not like buying a house. I've got a hefty sum available, but the owner finance deal I'd worked out sort of…hit a snag."

"Then you have a place in mind?"

More than in mind. "Yes." Taking in a deep breath, he had to believe what he was about to say would be well received. "As a matter of fact. I've been planning—"

The sound of Catherine's cell chirping in her pocket cut him off. Pulling her phone from her pocket, she took a step back. Frowning down at the number, she raised a finger at him. "Hello?"

"We've got a problem," the voice boomed. "Ted is refusing to do second chair. The client got wind of it, and I just spent over an hour reassuring him that you will be here to meet with him on Tuesday." The disgruntled voice was so loud Connor could hear every word without the aid of a speaker. "I've emailed you what little, updated information we have. I'll need you to—"

"No," she cut him off.

"What do you mean no? I haven't told you what I want yet."

"No, I will not be there on Tuesday." She took another step and shifted away from Connor. "Stacey nodded at me today."

"That's nice. Being my daughter will only get you so far, young lady—"

"Daddy. No."

"Listen." Even the man's heavy sigh could still be heard through the line. "You're not your mother. You don't belong in God's country. Neither does Stacey. There are people who deal with this sort of thing every day. They can sell the ranch and everything in it. If you want fresh air for Stacey we'll buy a country house, but it's time to come home."

Her free hand fisted at her side. "I'm not selling anything."

Four little words and Connor's hopes and dreams for Brennan's land shattered into painful shards of glass.

"I don't understand it, but I'm not leaving until I do. I'm

sorry, Daddy." Without another word, Catherine tapped the phone, placed it back in her pocket and, taking another step away, wrapped her arms around herself. Brushing away the evening chill, or perhaps something far cooler, she faced him again. "It's getting late."

And that was it. It was getting much later than she thought. Having put more distance between them Connor wasn't sure what hurt more, losing his stables or her.

CHAPTER FOURTEEN

"Well, good morning." Brooks waved his brother over. "Didn't expect to see you in town at this hour?"

Connor set his hat on the nearest rack and pulled up a chair at the round table. For the last two days since overhearing Catherine's call with her father, he'd been walking about with a cloud overhead, the only sunshine his time with Stacey, and when Finn said he needed some supplies from town, Connor sprang at the chance for a change of scenery. Lunch at the café was always a sure recipe to run into at least one of his brothers.

"You look tired." Toni, Brooks' fiancée, patted the empty seat next to her.

Meg, Adam's wife, was their waitress. "Iced tea?"

He'd have preferred something with a little bourbon in it, but that wouldn't go over well with his family or Abbie at this time of day. Not that the café owner served liquor anyhow, but she was almost as much of a mother hen as his aunt and her cronies, just a bit younger. "Sounds good."

Becky, Adam's veterinary assistant, smiled and wiggled her fingers at him the same way she had as a kid playing with his sister Grace. The same way she'd greet all the brothers. Except for Ethan. He actually merited a verbal greeting. Usually accompanied with a coy smile or some other youthful effort to capture his interest.

"Heard from Ethan lately?" he asked.

Becky looked around the table. "You're asking me?"

"Yeah," Connor nodded.

"If you guys haven't heard from him, why would I?" Her voice rose an octave higher than usual.

"I just figured y'all being . . . friends . . ." He didn't get to finish the sentence. Standing beside him, his sister-in-law kicked him, hard. "Ouch."

Shooting him a two-second glare that shouted think-twice-before-speaking-again with the same skill as his aunt, Meg addressed Becky. "Abbie says that Donna's about ready to come back to work from maternity leave. Guess she found someone to watch the baby?"

"Oh yeah." Becky's smile brightened at the change of subject and her tone seemed . . . relieved. Connor would have thought by now she'd have gotten used to the whole town knowing she was in love with his brother Ethan. "Her mom decided she could afford to take early retirement after all. This way Donna has daycare she can trust and Tuckers Bluff has a new job opening at the post office."

"That'll be a plum spot for someone," Meg added.

"Definitely. With you no longer filling in for Donna, you can open the B&B. It's almost ready, right?"

Meg grinned from ear to ear. "Pretty much. I'll do a grand opening celebration for the town folks first so everyone can see."

"Cool. Will you be joining us for girls' night tonight? We're heading to the Boots 'n Scoots."

Meg shook her head. "Too much to do still. What about tomorrow's poker game? You joining the ladies this week?"

"Maybe." Becky shrugged, then smiled. "Probably."

"She heard Aunt Eileen roped Ralph's granddaughter into joining the game. It's probably going to be the biggest game the social club has had since my wife came to town," Adam said, then stretched his hand out, snatched Meg's free hand and squeezed.

Meg laughed. "I'd better warn Frank to expect double his normal Saturday lunch crowd." Giving her husband's hand another squeeze, Meg darted off to the café kitchen.

"Well," D.J. smiled. "This will certainly give Frank something to grumble about for a week."

"Why is he such a sour puss?" Toni asked.

Brooks shrugged. "Must be a Marine thing."

On cue, D.J. and Connor both cleared their throats. Each having done their service to Uncle Sam in the Marines.

"Or not," Brooks smiled.

"Next time I'll update you on the merits of the Marine Corps, but I've got to head out." D.J. pushed his seat back. "Been here longer than I should have." On his feet he grabbed his hat and scanned the other side of the café. Spotting Abbie, he waited a moment for her to look his way, tipped his hat to her and smiled when she nodded and smiled back at him.

"I hate to say it," Becky stood, "but I should get back too. I promised Kelly I'd keep lunch short so she could leave early." She batted her eyes. "Hot date."

"At noon?" Toni asked.

"Nah. It's a dinner date, but you know, prep time." Shaking her head, Becky laughed. "If I had a figure like that woman the only thing I'd need to prep is . . ." Becky glanced at the men at the table and sighed. "Never mind. I gotta go."

"I'll walk you out," Toni said. "Sorry to eat and run, but I left dough rising and—"

Ignoring everyone else at the table, Brooks cut Toni off with a kiss. "See you later?"

"You bet." She smiled up at him.

Family dynamics had certainly shifted since Connor had last been home. "Looks like you're happy," he said to Brooks.

"Yeah." His eyes remained trained on Toni's departing form.

Connor glanced over at Adam, who was spying his wife serving a table of tourists passing through.

Maybe it was something in the water? He looked down at his drink. Or the iced tea. "How long did it take you to know?" he asked no one in particular.

Both brothers turned to face him.

He hadn't even realized he'd said the words out loud. Suddenly very conscious of where they were, he glanced around to see if anyone else had been within earshot. The only table close enough had plenty of dirty dishes but no people.

"Want to be a little more specific?" Brooks asked.

Adam chuckled. "Who is it?"

Brooks' brow buckled in confusion. "Who's who?"

"Oh, for heaven's sake," Adam rolled his eyes. "Did you really think you and I would be the only two Farradays to fall in love?"

"Wait a minute." Connor put up his hands. "No one has said anything about love."

"Sure you did." Adam waved one hand at him. "You asked when did we know. Or were you talking about Becky crushing on Ethan?"

"We really should stop picking on the poor kid for that." Brooks shrugged. "She stopped asking us about him every chance she gets years ago." Adam lifted a brow at him and Brooks' mouth fell open. "Is she still asking you about him?"

Adam's head bobbed. "Not as much and," he turned to Connor, "in all fairness she asks about you a lot too, but still."

"Me?" Connor asked a bit surprised at the idea. "Why?"

"Probably because you, Ethan, and Grace are the three siblings who don't live in town. Besides, it's less obvious when she's asking about Ethan if she tacks you and Gracie into the mix."

Brooks shook his head. "Damn. We sound like the old ladies in the social club."

Before anyone could crack a joke about gossiping women, D.J. came marching back inside, hat in hand, and made a beeline straight to the table. A man on a mission and the hackles on Connor's neck rose. From the way Brooks stared their police chief brother down, he wasn't expecting good news either.

Adam shifted in place, sitting straighter, ready to pounce if needed. "What's up?"

Shaking his head, D.J. blew out a clearly frustrated breath. "Just got pinged. The blood tests are in on Jake Thomas."

"And?" Brooks prompted.

"Clean. No drugs."

Adam leaned on an elbow. "I'm not sure if that's bad or good news."

"Fighting an addiction isn't easy, but sometimes it's easier than fixing mean," D.J. answered.

Brooks bobbed his head and Connor could almost see his thoughts running in a hundred different directions. Hopefully one of those thoughts would figure out what had gone so God-awful wrong with Jake Thomas. And though he wasn't happy to hear about the trouble in the Thomas marriage, he was at least glad the conversation had drifted away from his love life. Or lack of one.

Connor wasn't ready to think about love. And certainly not with a woman he'd known less than a week and who came fully equipped with a five-year-old daughter and plenty of baggage. And yet, the last few evenings when Catherine had come by to pick up Stacey, there was only one thing he was positive about—he wasn't sure of a damn thing.

● ● ●

At first Catherine had been a bit hesitant to take Eileen up on her offer to keep an eye on Stacey in the afternoons so she could get through her grandfather's things sooner, but even if her daughter still wasn't nodding or smiling at Catherine, she was different. Lighter. Happier. Catherine could tell, and after almost two years of a sullen, lost child, she simply couldn't deny Stacey afternoons coloring and baking with the closest thing to a grandmother she'd ever know.

Catherine just wished she understood what the hell was going on with Connor. For a couple of days now he'd kept his distance. Which was her own fault. She hadn't reacted well after the kiss. Frankly, she'd been almost as startled by the action as the reaction. But she hadn't meant to completely turn him away. At least she didn't think she had. Now she'd yet to find a place or excuse to talk to him about it, so all she got from him was a nod or wave from across the room. Sitting at the opposite end of the dinner table from her, he'd only speak if someone else started the conversation. The only responses she got were a nod or a shake of the head.

"Stacey helped with the blueberry pies." Eileen waved at two pies cooling near the window sill.

The delicious aroma of fresh baked goods had hit Catherine the second she'd walked in the door. "Smells wonderful. Where's Stacey?"

Eileen's gaze darted to the rear door and back. "Connor took her to pick some peas for me from the garden."

"Oh." Catherine sneaked a peek out the window and resisted the idea of volunteering to go help her daughter. And Connor.

If only she could get that damn kiss out of her head. Her grandfather hadn't thrown a single piece of paper out since the day he took over the ranch from his daddy. And he hadn't sorted or filed a blessed thing in what seemed like forever. As much attention and concentration as it required to sort through all of that, every so often she'd find herself thinking of Connor's arms around her waist, the weight of his hands on her bottom, the feel of his lips maneuvering across hers. Then she'd snap out of her reverie and realize she'd made more of a mess with the filing system than what she'd started with.

A pea filled bucket in her hand, Stacey appeared smiling at the back door, her knees covered in dirt, and her shirt dusty, and Catherine wondered what kind of garden Aunt Eileen had.

Smiling behind her daughter, Connor came in equally covered in dirt and dust and all Catherine could think of was how much fun it would be to strip him out of those soiled clothes. *Blast.*

Connor had said he was sorry for kissing her. She wasn't quite sure if he was being gallant, or if he truly regretted getting involved with her. Not that one kiss was involved, but usually one kiss led to another, and then more kisses led to more touching until two people wound up hot and sweaty under the sheets. She didn't think there was a man alive who didn't want to get hot and sweaty with a woman. Any woman. Then again, maybe women like her only appealed to men in suits.

"I'll take those. You two go wash up." Eileen received the peas from Stacey and then grinned at her nephew. But the part that had Catherine debating what to do with their lives after the funeral Sunday was the brief smile Stacey flashed at Ms. Eileen.

"I should go help her," Catherine turned to follow Stacey.

"No need." Eileen offered a reassuring smile. "I laid clean clothes on the bed. I hope you don't mind. I found a few more things in the trunks."

Catherine shook her head. In her normal world it would never have occurred to her to accept hand me downs. Graciously or otherwise. But here, where her daughter lit up like the proverbial Christmas tree at the site of pink cowboy boots and a tiny, silver-buckled belt for worn blue jeans, the more the better. "Thank you."

Connor circled wide around the room and Catherine stepped back. She'd give him all the space he needed, at least while she figured out what to do with Stacey. And once she knew how long she'd be staying in Tuckers Bluff, maybe she'd have some clue what to do with Connor Farraday.

CHAPTER FIFTEEN

"You're going to have to tell her mama what you're up to." Sean Farraday poured himself a tall glass of milk to go with the eggs and pancakes on his plate.

"Not yet." Eileen chimed in. "Catherine is still too skittish on ranch life. She'd pack that child up and fly her home in a heartbeat if she knew what Connor was doing."

Sean stabbed a forkful of scrambled eggs. "That's her right. It's her child."

Eileen turned to Connor. "What do you think?"

"I think it's easier to ask forgiveness than permission." Connor reached for the bowl of grits. "But Dad's right. I can't keep this up forever. I thought for sure Catherine was going to figure out we weren't just picking peas last night when she saw how dirty we were."

Coming in late from his Saturday morning routine, Finn nodded at everyone, grabbed a plate from the counter, and joined them at the table.

Sean picked up the conversation, "I gather yesterday went well?"

The vision of little Stacey grinning over her shoulder at him every time they rounded a barrel had him smiling from the inside out. "Better than well. Stacey loves everything about the horses." And he'd really liked having her riding in his lap. "Of course we've barely worked our way up to a trot, but every time we turned around she reached for the flag." That smiling face would be permanently seared in his memory. "She really loves it."

"And you think that's why she's smiling at us." Sean set his empty glass in the sink.

"I do. Think about it. Part of Stacey's problem stems from a loss of control after the accident. Among other things, she couldn't wake up her daddy. Riding with me, holding the reins, it's very liberating for a small child to be able to control a thousand-pound horse. She's gone from quiet and sullen to smiling when she's with the horses, and now you've seen how often she smiles at us."

"And she's humming more." Finn reached for a biscuit and noticed everyone looking at him. "What? I like the kid. She's cute. And yeah, she seems to be more comfortable around here."

"I have to admit," Eileen glanced toward the front of the house where Catherine and Stacey would be arriving any minute, "even I didn't expect to see this much change so fast."

"I did." Connor waved his fork at no one in particular. "I've been reading up on horse therapy and it really is fantastic how caring for and riding horses can help people with anything from a physical impairment to emotional challenges. Kids, adults, the stats are impressive."

Sean nodded. "So what's the plan today?"

"I thought I'd let her sit her own horse. I'll lead her around. Walk the course. See how she does."

"Which horse?" his dad asked.

"The Palomino. Princess."

Sean nodded. "Good choice."

Midair Aunt Eileen's fork froze. "Wouldn't a pony be better?"

"Nope. Ponies can be little shits." Connor smiled. "Princess is small for a quarter horse at barely fourteen hands so she's a good size for a first ride."

"That mare is as docile as they come, Eileen. All the kids love her," Sean agreed. "But I still say you need to tell her mother. Have you thought about the liability if something happens to her?"

"Sean. Don't even think it." Aunt Eileen waved her fork at him.

"Don't look at me like that. All the kids fell off everything from sheep to horses more than once around here, and they're still with us. But you know as well as I do, what Connor's doing isn't just a little horsemanship. He's teaching that little thing to participate in the Ranchathon with kids who were weaned on these animals, and I don't know of a ranch kid alive who came out of weeks of practicing without at least a scratch."

Aunt Eileen pressed her lips together and turned to Connor, her eyes slowly narrowing. "Promise me you won't let anything— anything at all—happen to that child."

How the hell was he supposed to promise something like that?

"Come on, Aunt Eileen." Finn reached for a glass of juice. "It's not like Connor's putting her in a bull chute at the rodeo. He's being as careful as he can and, not that anyone has asked me, but I agree with you and Connor. The way that sprig has caught on to handling horses, she'll be able to tell her mother for herself what they've been up to."

Their father shook his head and pushed away from the table. "It's up to you, son, but you'd better keep in mind, there ain't nothing stupider than tangling with a mama's cub." Sean Farraday locked gazes with Connor long enough to make sure he'd gotten his point across then reached for his hat. "I've got to get back to work."

Finn turned to his brother, shrugged, then pushed to his feet. "Wait up, Dad, I'll come with you."

The doorbell rang at the same time the front door squeaked open and tiny footsteps clacked across the hardwood floor, her mother's heavier step following. Holding a new drawing of what he suspected was supposed to be his bay, Pharaoh, Stacey tugged at his sleeve.

Crouching down, he scooped her up into his arms. "What have we got here?"

Sporting a wide, toothy grin, she pressed the picture in front of his face and with his free hand, he accepted the precious gift.

"The best picture of Pharaoh I've ever seen. Thank you, sweetie." Turning the picture to show Catherine and his aunt, alarm prickled the hairs on the back of his neck at the wide-eyed expressions staring back at him. Quickly looking back at Stacey he eased her away, checking to see if perhaps he had scratched her with his buckle or maybe gripped her too hard. Not seeing anything, his gaze shot up to her still smiling face. Nothing out of place. So what had her mother and his aunt looking at her as if they'd seen the Ghost of Christmas Past? "What's wrong?"

Aunt Eileen shook her head and rather than say anything, a whisper of a smile slowly took over her face.

Totally confused, Connor looked to Catherine.

"She," Catherine sucked in a slow breath and blew it back out, "she wanted you to pick her up."

Connor nodded.

"She tugged on your arm."

He nodded again, not grasping what Catherine was . . . and then it hit him. He'd never seen Stacey reach out for what she wanted. Not only didn't she *verbally* ask for things, she never asked for anything in any way. Never pointed to what she wanted. Most of the time her mother and his aunt and anyone else who talked to her had to guess and hope they'd gotten it right.

Holy crap, this was huge. His cheeks pulled with sheer joy.

Oh yeah, no way Catherine could be mad at him when he finally told her what he was up to. Maybe.

• • •

Between Eileen's casual banter and stories of Grace, the youngest Farraday's barrel racing days, and Catherine's wandering thoughts on how much Stacey had opened up since arriving in West Texas, the drive into town with Eileen for the Tuckers Bluff Ladies Afternoon Social Club gathering had felt much shorter than her initial drive from town to the ranch last Sunday afternoon.

Settled at a back table at the Silver Spurs Café, Catherine still didn't quite understand why a group that met once a week on a Saturday morning was an afternoon club, but who was she to question what had apparently been a tradition for longer than she'd been alive.

"You should try one of Toni's cake balls. They're fantastic." Aunt Eileen dealt another round of face down cards. "Though she doesn't put as much booze in them for the café."

"She doesn't put as much booze in them for anyone anymore." Sally May peeked at the newly dealt card.

"I guess it was a little bit much that night." Dorothy chuckled under breath. "But we sure did have a good time."

"Too good." Waiting for her next card, Becky, Dorothy's granddaughter, shook her head. "I get there to pick you up, expecting to find a few friends having fun in a card game, but no. There's a dead man in the barn and four of you are as high as kites thanks to sauced cake balls, singing really strange songs, and laughing so hard I'm surprised y'all weren't peeing in your pants."

Dead man in the barn? Catherine scanned the table. One of the ladies fiddled with her chips, another took a sip of her drink, a couple more looked from one card to another, one with a frown and one with a smile. But no one seemed at all affected by talk of a dead body during a poker game. "Dare I ask?"

Eileen glanced in her direction. "Oh, well."

Dorothy shook her head at her granddaughter.

"Long story," Sally May added, unconcerned with the conversation and tossed a chip in the pot. "I'm in."

"Not me." Dorothy scooped her cards together. The three of clubs, eight of diamonds, and king of hearts showing was a less-than- hopeful hand, and clearly, the facedown cards weren't going to change that. "No point in pretending with this mess."

Catherine waited for someone to please explain the dead body to her. A dead body on the ranch where her daughter was now being cared for by a man who hadn't said more than two words to her in about as many days.

Smiling as she peeked under the uncovered cards, Eileen nodded her head. "I'm in." Then she turned to Catherine. "Sad situation, Toni's soon to be ex-husband was spying on her when a tree branch fell on him."

"Killed him instantly," Dorothy said.

"Broke his neck," Sally May added helpfully.

Catherine looked to Becky who tossed a chip into the middle of the table, announced she was in, and then turned to Catherine. "Truth is he was an abusive jerk, but I suspect had they not been tanked on Toni's extra-juiced desserts, things might been a bit more . . . respectful."

"Respectful my ass." Sally May shook her head. "Men like that deserve to have their privates tarred and feathered."

"Often," Dorothy added.

And they all seemed like such nice, sweet ladies when the game had first started.

"Sorry I'm late." A curvaceous younger woman hurried around to an empty seat and glanced in Catherine's direction. "I'm Kelly."

"Nice to meet you. I'm Catherine."

"So?" Becky looked expectantly at the newcomer.

"Not much to tell." Kelly set her purse down and began counting out chips. "The guy had plenty of rhythm on the dance floor. We scooted around for hours. Conversation wasn't bad either. I was a little worried that he still lived at home, but in these parts . . ."

Becky and a few women nodded as if the explanation made perfect sense and didn't need finishing.

"I detect another 'but' coming," Eileen said.

"Yep. The guy kisses like a drowning fish."

"How can a fish drown?" Dorothy stopped shuffling the spare deck.

"I don't know, but he kissed like it. He was sloppy and slobbery and his lips were all over the place. Not in a good way either. I couldn't figure out if he was trying to suck in air or latch on to his mama's teets."

"Eww." Becky shuddered in her seat.

"Yeah. That about covers it."

"Well, if he's a nice man..." Dorothy returned to shuffling, but every adult head at the table turned to face her with mirrored expressions.

"Don't be ridiculous, Dorothy. If the man can't kiss he won't be any use to her in bed, and if there's no getting a few good years in bed out of a man, what's the point of having one?"

This was so not the conversation Catherine had expected to have.

"Don't you agree?" Sally May looked straight at Catherine.

What the hell did she know? Instantly her mind flipped over to the one and only kiss she and Connor had shared. Yeah, she wouldn't object to finding out what else those lips could do. Instantly, heat rushed to her cheeks.

"See," Sally May said, "Catherine agrees with me."

"I'd be more worried about the lives at home part." Dorothy set the fresh deck aside.

"Why?" Eileen cut the cards. "Finn and Connor live at home."

"Well, of course, Finn lives at home, even if he is the younger brother, that boy has been destined to run that ranch since he sat his first horse."

A broad grin spread across Eileen's face. "He really did shine as the heir apparent regardless of birth order."

"And Connor's mostly lived away for years. Only reason he's back now is to buy the—" Sally May stopped suddenly, looking down to the floor and frowning up at Eileen, who was sitting ramrod straight.

Catherine almost smiled watching the antics. These ladies were indeed an interesting bunch.

"He's wanting to buy his own horse ranch," Eileen finished Sally May's sentence.

"Yes," Catherine nodded. "He's mentioned that."

"He has?" Eileen's voice rose slightly and Sally May shot her friend a look that could have meant anything from I-told-you-so to what's-your-problem, and Catherine didn't know enough about either of these ladies to even venture a guess.

"Yes, he's been working in oil to save up."

"Started at the fields." Eileen examined her cards. "Moved to the offshore rigs not long ago. Made more money that way."

"I guess it's expensive to buy enough land for a ranch?"

"Depends on where you're buying and what you're buying," Dorothy put in. "Is there water or a creek nearby? That's gonna cost more because we don't have that many creeks running through these parts. Are you in a grassy part of the state or dry? Some places where the grass is plenty you can raise a cow on an acre of land. Further into this side of the state, a rancher could need a hundred acres. It all varies and it all effects price."

"What's going to cost Connor big is good stock. A good horse can cost a small fortune. He's already picked up a couple, but for his plans, he needs more."

"And that costs." Catherine thought she got it.

"Big time," Becky chimed in, then shrugged. "At a veterinary clinic, you hear people talking about more than hoof in mouth. Some of the prices the ranchers buy and sell their stud bulls for is mind boggling."

"So all that's holding up Connor from his own ranch is finding the right place?"

All eyes at the table turned to her. Not the same way they had when they were explaining the differences between seven-card stud and Texas hold'em, but more like they knew something she didn't. And that had her nearly squirming in her seat. Silly. Ridiculous actually. But uncomfortable nonetheless.

"You planning on staying on long after the funeral tomorrow?" Sally May asked and this time Catherine felt the movement under the table at Eileen's booted toe connecting with Sally May's foot.

"I think so."

All heads turned to her.

"My, uh, daughter is really liking it here. A lot will depend on my work." Assuming she even has a job when she doesn't show up on Tuesday.

All heads nodded, slowly returning their attention to the cards on the table. Hairs on the back of Catherine's neck were beginning to prickle. Call it crazy or call it paranoid or call it gut instinct, but these women definitely knew something she didn't, and she damn well wanted to find out what the hell it was.

CHAPTER SIXTEEN

Scanning the cavernous space, Connor recognized every citizen over the age of thirty-five. Everyone and anyone who would remember Old Man Brennan came to his funeral.

The pews weren't completely full, but darn close. Growing up, Sunday mornings and church had been a family ritual. Button-down shirts and pressed pants, the family climbed into the massive Suburban, then filed into the historic building and took up an entire row.

The regulars with the large brood of kids always had what seemed like reserved seats. Third row from the front, left side was the Farraday pew. The Sullivans, the Bradys, the Rankins all had their own pews. Ranch families tended to have the most children. The dads had easily teased about free labor. The bigger the ranch, the more hands needed. As a kid, before he was old enough to be of any real help, he'd learned what to do by watching Adam and Brooks before him. His older brothers were two years apart but there were only thirteen months between him and Brooks.

D.J. came to his side. Feet set slightly apart, hands clasped behind his back, he was at parade rest. Something that came naturally for a man who had served his four years in the Marine Corps and the remainder of his life on a police force. "I still don't like funerals."

Connor nodded. None of them did. The memories of his mother were few and far between, but the ones he had were cherished and nurtured and seared into his mind and heart. Sometimes on a clear and windy day, if he stood in just the right spot and looked to the sprawling, old oak tree where he and his brothers would find a million ways to get into trouble, Connor could hear his mom calling them in for supper. Adam, Brookstone, Connor, Declan, Ethan. Supper and Sunday mornings were always a time for their full, given names. On those days they were getting into trouble they were reminded of the complete names printed on their birth certificates: Adam Sean, Brookstone Ryan, Connor Mathew, Declan James, Ethan Patrick. At only three when his mama passed, Finn had not been old enough to have had the pleasure of hearing his mother stand, feet spread, hands fisted on her waist, reciting the roll call of names. Though Aunt Eileen had done an excellent job of rounding up Finnegan George and Grace Maureen.

There hadn't been a single funeral he'd attended in the last twenty-plus years that didn't leave him with a knot in his throat, an ache in his heart, and the sound of his mother's voice in his ears. "*I love you, baby boy.*" They'd all been her baby boys.

"It's never easy." Sean Patrick Farraday came up beside his two sons. "Catherine and Stacey are here. Aunt Eileen rode in with her."

"I thought you were bringing her?"

"She insisted on driving herself. Eileen did her magic and finagled a ride."

Connor felt the smile tug at his cheeks. "Aunt Eileen is pretty good at finagling."

"That she is." His father nodded. "That she is."

From where he stood in the vestibule, Connor could see Catherine just inside the church doors, leaning over and talking to Stacey. The little girl wasn't responding, her gaze frozen forward. She reminded him too much of how she'd been those first few days at the ranch. And he didn't like it one damn bit. Stacey apparently didn't care much for funerals either. Two steps forward. One step back.

Noting the increasingly pasty, white tone Catherine's complexion took on with every step, Connor was torn between rushing forward to render aid, any aid, and staying put and minding his place. The second she stepped into the aisle,

Catherine's gaze shot straight to the front of the church. The target of her intense, pain-filled gaze, the simple coffin Ralph had picked out and paid for years ago. Place be damned.

• • •

Squeezing Stacey's hand a little tighter than she should have, Catherine made her way slowly up the aisle. The pastor had explained the front rows would be saved for family. She'd done her best to explain that she and Stacey were all the family there was. Grandpa's only brother had died in one of the wars. Never married. There might have been a sister, she wasn't sure. Both she and her mother had been only children. Only daughters. And now here Catherine was with her only baby.

Halfway up the aisle, she could hear the hushed murmurs of more people arriving, and yet the pews already appeared filled. How many people had her grandfather known? Had all these people cared about him? A muffled sniffle caught her ear and she turned to her left. An older lady Catherine had never met held a hanky to her eyes. A large man who showed the pride and strength of years of working the land, comforted her with a tender arm around her shoulder. A few rows up she saw more sets of eyes glimmering with sadness. The ache at the loss was still there, but somehow not quite as sharp.

At the front of the church she spotted the requisite two empty pews. Her heart sank at the isolation of her and Stacey alone in a sea of people. A family of two. Not til she'd guided her daughter into place and heard the low, rumbly voice urging her to scoot over had she realized Connor had shadowed her into the pew.

Blinking up at him, her feet remained in place, her mind desperately relaying instructions to her uncooperative limbs.

"Just a little further," he whispered near her ear.

She'd taken a couple more steps when she spotted Sean Farraday and Aunt Eileen coming toward her from the opposite side of the pews. Nestled between Connor and his parents,

Catherine and Stacey were not alone.

The sounds of more footsteps drew near. More guests. Softly the organ music began to play. Or had it been playing all along? The heavy footfalls eased almost beside her. Turning her head, she glanced over her shoulder. Single file, the remainder of the Farraday clan shuffled into the row behind her. Adam standing in the aisle ushering Finn, Brooks, Toni, Meg and then taking his place at the edge of the pew.

No. In Tuckers Bluff no Brennan would stand alone.

The preacher's words, Sean Farraday's eulogy, and all the condolences swam in the foggy recesses of Catherine's mind. If anyone asked her how she'd gotten from the front of the church to this large room filled with tables, chairs, people, and enough food to feed half the state, she wouldn't be able to say.

"You look like you could use a little fresh air." Connor's voice broke through the haze.

That sounded wonderful. But blinking twice, she scanned the room from left to right.

"Stacey's with Toni."

Catherine's gaze settled on her little girl, her hand encased in the protective care of a lovely blonde. Toni. The woman whose other hand was equally and lovingly encased in the hand of another Farraday son.

"I don't understand. Holding hands with your aunt makes sense, but we hardly know Brooks' . . ." Catherine was at a loss for the exact relationship the pair had, though obviously close and in love. Catherine had noticed early on that everyone was given a label; Adam's wife, Brooks' nurse, Eileen's friend, but Toni, she'd been introduced as Meg's old friend when any idiot could see the greater attachment was to Brooks.

"In an effort to make friends, Toni explained she was having a baby. That appears to have created an instant bond between them."

"And would explain why my daughter is staring at Toni's flat tummy."

Connor chuckled. "I suppose."

"She must not be far along."

"Not very." He gently cupped her elbow. "There's a really nice garden this way."

Confident Stacey was in good hands, Catherine followed Connor's lead. "Oh, wow."

The small courtyard was a botanical haven in the middle of barren cattle country. A thick green lawn sprawled to shrub-lined fences with a variety of colored vines and splashes of bright blooms. In the center, a massive oak tree created a shady canopy over a curved stone bench.

"It's hard to not feel at peace here," Connor nudged her toward the tree.

"Thank you." Catherine lowered herself to the stone bench. "I needed this."

"I figured." Connor sat beside her. "I considered sneaking you a glass of sacramental wine. Father Tim probably wouldn't have noticed, but as sure as her name is Eileen Callahan, my aunt would have found me out."

"That's okay. I'm more of a white wine girl."

Connor bobbed his head and Catherine had the feeling he was committing it to memory.

"Reading some of Mom's stories reminded me of how much I loved to write when I was young."

"That's nice. A connection with your mom."

That's what she'd thought. "I wrote a story yesterday." Why had she shared that?

"Really?" One corner of his mouth curled upward in a lazy smile all the brothers seemed to have, but only Connor's had a way of making her almost fluster.

"Really. Nothing for a Pulitzer prize."

"What's it about?"

Well, she couldn't very well say nothing now. She had been the one to bring it up. "A girl's first kiss."

The lazy smile spread to full blown and Catherine's stomach did a somersault. "Tell me about it."

Served her right. "I don't even think it was that good."

"The story or the kiss?" Eyes bright with amusement twinkled back at her.

"It's fiction."

"Uh huh."

"It is." She resisted the urge to cross her arms and stomp her feet. "Trust me. Most first kiss stories are a blip on the radar. Unless an author is writing humor about locked braces, they're rarely worth writing about."

"I don't know."

"You remember your first kiss?"

Connor nodded. "You?"

"You go first."

"So you do remember?"

She didn't stomp her feet, but she did cross her arms.

"Patty Cantrel," he said. "It was behind the barn after the annual Ranchathon." Connor paused to glance away and smile, then look back. "I'd finaled in all the events that day. Was thrilled. Patty congratulated me, and puckering my lips I gave her some good old sugar." His smile widened. "I was eight."

Catherine laughed. That wasn't what she'd expected. "Started chasing skirts young. "

Hefting a shoulder, Connor shook his head. "Not really. We all dated a little in high school, but I think Brooks was the first with the rule of not dating a local girl. At least not after high school. He'd dated a gal who worked the café at the time. After he broke up we all got the worst service. Often wondered if she'd spit in our food, too. That rule made a lot of sense."

"Does it still?"

"It's worked well so far." Connor tipped his head back for a better look at her eyes. "What about you? First kiss."

Catherine rolled her eyes. "I'd hoped you'd forget about that."

"That bad?"

"That unmemorable. Johnny Tallon. Seventh grade. I'd developed rather well at an early age and someone dared him to kiss me. He didn't have a clue what he was doing." A little chuckle escaped. "Fortunately for him, neither did I."

"That's a shame."

"Are you saying Patty Cantrel rocked your world at age eight?"

Connor shook his head laughing. "Honestly, neither of us could figure out why all those people on TV wanted to kiss so much."

"I'd say you figured it out." Open mouth, insert foot. Why was she being so blasted honest with him?

"You would, huh?" One brow rose high on his forehead and that earlier twinkle in his eye reappeared.

Oh, what the hell. She nodded.

Connor's attention shifted to some distant spot then back again. His hand moved on top of hers and those blasted sparks of anticipation shot up her back and down again, settling low in her already fluttering belly. Closing his eyes, he sucked in a deep breath, then his gaze bore into hers. "So would I."

One hand remained at his side. The other clung to hers. Only his mouth touched hers. A soft, sweet kiss that had her breath catching and her insides melting into a puddle of wanton mush. Only his lips had her heart racing and her mind empty. Only his lips started the signs of a four-alarm fire. Only his kiss. And all too soon, those delicious lips eased away. Her chest heaving in large gulps of air, lifted and dropped in rhythm with his deep, long breaths.

His forehead leaned against hers and he squeezed her hand. "If Aunt Eileen will babysit, would you do me the honor of joining me for dinner tonight?"

Catherine nodded, their foreheads still touching.

"And maybe a little dancing?"

She nodded again. She didn't think he had the same kind of dance in mind she did. Then again, maybe he did.

CHAPTER SEVENTEEN

A date. A real live date. Not a pickup in a local bar. Not one of the many groupies of sorts who hung out waiting to spend a little—or a lot—of time with one of the men who had worked hard for weeks and was ready to play hard. He was doing dinner and dancing West Texas-style with Catherine Hammond.

It took a moment for Connor to shake his thoughts loose. He wasn't a damn teenager. Neither was she. Unlike a big city where he could stop at the supermarket and pick up a small bouquet of roses, his only choice was to snip a few of his aunt's blooms. No big deal. Even if he was trying to impress a city girl. And like it or not, he wanted to make a good impression. A really good one.

Sucking in a deep breath, he rapped on the door and waited what seemed like too much time for Catherine to open it. The deep furrow between her brow and the way she hurried him inside didn't bode well.

"Stacey's not feeling well." She turned and scurried quickly down the hall to the room they were staying in.

"What's wrong?" Connor had to shorten his stride not to reach the room before her.

"I don't know. Something she ate. Maybe a bug. I was stepping out of the shower . . ."

Connor's mind almost wandered off into its own little version of Catherine stark naked in droplets of water when he shoved the inappropriate thoughts back and his gaze landed on the little girl curled up in bed, a trash can at her side.

"She threw up at my feet. I should have known she wasn't feeling well. She'd been so pale. But," Catherine sighed, "I guess I just thought if she didn't feel well she might actually say something, so I… I didn't pay enough attention."

"I can call Brooks. He'll come take a look." Connor inched closer to the bed, and ran his hand along the downy curls. Stacey didn't move. Her eyes closed. "She's sleeping."

"I think so. She's been calm for almost twenty minutes. I guess exhaustion finally won."

"That's a good sign." He pulled out his phone to send for his brother, and Catherine's arm shot out. Fingers seared his skin through his sleeve with the same intensity of branding iron.

"Don't. If she's stopped, she's doing better."

"You sure?" He held his phone out and smiled. "Brooks loves to save the day."

He was rewarded with a whisper of a smile. "I'm sure."

"We'll still have to make sure she doesn't dehydrate."

Catherine's eyes widened in surprise. "You know about kids and stomachaches?"

"Not exactly." If he weren't so worried about Stacey, he might have laughed. "My brother is a doctor, my aunt is a nurturer, I have four younger siblings, and animal husbandry is a great way to learn all the facts of life."

"I see." Catherine nodded and looked to her daughter. "I don't think—"

"Of course not," Connor cut her off. "For now we should probably let her sleep."

Catherine nodded.

"There has to be a good flick on TV." He headed for the pantry to see what old Ralph had in stock that would be good for a kid with an upset tummy. "Here we go. Saltines, and," he glanced about, "ginger ale. The magic elixir." He grabbed both and backed out of the closet. "And I'll call my aunt. When Stacey's tummy settles, I'm betting Aunt Eileen has some chicken broth in the freezer for just such an occasion."

"My daughter getting sick?"

"Anyone getting sick. Chicken soup is the cure-all for whatever ails you."

Catherine's gaze shifted to the guestroom door. "That sounds like a plan. I'm sorry to have upset yours."

Offering a reassuring smile, Connor shook his head. "I'm just sorry she's not feeling well. It's not fun."

"Well. Plan B. I have a ton of fresh leftovers in the fridge. Do you have a preference? King Ranch Casserole." She stuck her head in fridge. "Chicken Cordon Bleu Casserole."

Her rounded rear end waved at him like a red flag taunting a bull.

"I can't see what this one says. Something with Mac and Cheese."

"King Ranch is fine." Anything was fine if she'd get her head out of the fridge and straighten up. "I'll set the table."

"I'll just stick this in the microwave."

She stared at the microwave as the timer ticked down. "Aunt Eileen and the other ladies said you worked oil rigs for years to save money."

He nodded. Not new information.

The timer rang and she eased the dish out and set it on the counter. "They say it was very dangerous."

Connor retrieved a handful of silverware from the drawers. He considered toning it down, but he didn't want to lie. "It is."

Uncovering the casserole, she nibbled on her lower lip. "If it was so dangerous, why did you do it?"

He'd have loved to have said for the money, and it was, but there was more to it. "I loved it. The excitement, the challenges, the rush."

"And you don't get that from ranching." She set the dish on a trivet.

"Sometimes. It's different. Not for everyone." He set two plates beside the silverware.

"And you're leaving it behind for horses?"

He smiled at her. "Horses have always been the goal."

"Yes," she nodded. "You don't think you'll be bored in comparison?"

"Not for a minute." He moved the dish to the table and wondered what all the questions were about. Working with horses was an entirely different kind of thrill. Like kissing Catherine.

Catherine got the glasses and a bottle of wine from the fridge. "This okay?"

Without really looking he nodded. Anything to keep her out of that fridge. Seated across from Catherine, Connor dug into his food and did his best to wipe his mind of all images that had nothing to do with a chicken casserole.

"Then I don't have to worry about you falling off and breaking your neck and never seeing you again." Catherine dangled a forkful of noodle in front of her. "I mean…"

Connor covered her hand with his. "I'm not going to break my neck."

"But those horses are so . . . big."

"Has anyone ever told you that you worry too much?"

Catherine sputtered a laugh. "In my line of work, worrying means taking care of business."

"Well, you don't have to worry about me. No more dangerous work for me. You're only job is making sure your daughter gets better, and if I were a betting man, I'd say it was just something she ate."

"That would be best case scenario. There were a lot of sweets this afternoon."

"Yeah," she smiled. "There were."

Her cheeks turned a delectable shade of pink. Connor set his fork on his plate, pulled out his phone, swiped to an app, clicked, and set the apparatus down as Shania Twain's "You're Still the One" played into the room. He pushed to his feet, skirted the edge of the table, and bowing slightly at the waist, extended his hand to her.

More pink filled her cheeks as she stood and accepted his hand. In an easy twirl she curled into his arms for a lazy two-step around the kitchen. Somewhere around verse two or three, he was getting high on the gentle feel of her when she leaned in a bit more. Another chorus and her head eased against his shoulder. He could easily do this the rest of the night.

The faster beat of Vince Gil's "Feels Like Love" kicked in and loosening his hold, Connor led her into an honest to goodness two-step, circling the spacious kitchen. Spinning her out and winding her back in he relished the soft giggle.

"I'll have you know I've always had two left feet. Maybe three." She smiled up at him.

"Could have fooled me." He twirled her once again and didn't mind at all when the next tune on his play list turned out to be yet another upbeat dance song. It gave his head time to clear. Time to think. Time to realize that he still didn't know her plans for the ranch and she still didn't know his intentions for it either. If he didn't speak up soon this would be a rocky road between them. But right now, tonight, none of his plans seemed as important as making Catherine Hammond smile.

• • •

"I'm selfish enough to admit I love having a little one in the house again." Aunt Eileen smiled at Catherine from across the Farraday kitchen table. "And I'm so glad to see her feeling so much better. Poor thing looked so pitiful last night when I brought over the soup."

"Thank you. I really appreciate your taking the time to come over. I have to admit it was incredibly reassuring having you there to back up my diagnosis."

"That's what friends are for, dear. Once her tummy was empty she just needed a little rehydration and nourishment. Today she's already right as rain."

Catherine wondered how much help her neighbors in Chicago would have been. Though she and David had little time to offer them more than a nod and a smile, after the accident she'd been showered with food and the sporadic comforting word, but she doubted an upset tummy would have garnered the same attention.

"And," Eileen continued, "she does seem to be coming out of her shell. Don't you think?"

"I'm not sure if I should credit the time you've spent doing all the things I'm sure my grandmother would have done with me, or the quiet, West Texas air, or a combination of both. But either way, I know I need to stay here a little longer and find out. Let whatever's happening play out. See if Stacey continues to improve."

And if her daughter did show more signs of becoming the bright-eyed child she once was, Catherine would need to consider how returning to Chicago would change things. Would all the newly made progress remain in West Texas the way the old Stacey seemed to still be trapped in the automobile wreckage on a dark suburban Chicago street.

"She does seem to love it here." Aunt Eileen glanced at the little girl happily drawing away at the large square coffee table in the other room. "So you're thinking of staying permanently at the ranch?"

"I don't know about that. My life is in Chicago." Assuming she hadn't shot her career in the foot regardless of who her father was. "But we have all summer to figure it out."

Aunt Eileen lit up. "So the plan is to stay the summer. And then…sell?" The woman watched her carefully over the rim of her teacup.

"Maybe." But the longer Catherine stayed, the more she uncovered of her family history, the less inclined she was to let go of the last tangible connection she had to her roots. "I thought I'd look into what it would take to keep the ranch as a summer home. Continue to lease the lands to your family, if you'd like to continue, but come out to the house for vacation time."

Eileen nodded slowly, her eyes narrowed in thought. For the life of her, Catherine couldn't tell if they were good or bad thoughts, but regardless, she felt like the woman was privy to something she wasn't.

"Oh good." A glint in her eyes, Eileen slapped her hands

together. "You'll definitely be here for the Ranchathon?"

"When is it again?"

"Two Saturdays from now. Families come from all over the county. It's like a mini rodeo. All the ranchers around here get to strut their stuff and battle for bragging rights to best whatever until next year's Ranchathon."

"Really. I thought it was just for the children?"

Eileen shook her head. "Dear, did no one ever teach you the only thing that separates the men from the boys is the price of their toys?"

Before she could stop it a tiny rumble in her gut rose, bursting out a laugh. "No." Catherine held her hand to her mouth, in a vague effort to slow her mirth. "That is pretty funny."

"What is?" Connor came in the back door and hung his hat.

Aunt Eileen's eyes rounded, her brows arched high and her shoulders lifted and fell in a casual shrug. "Just girl talk."

Connor's gaze shifted from his aunt to Catherine and back. Shaking his head, he'd clearly made up his mind that whether he believed his aunt or not, he had no intention of venturing down that particular rabbit hole.

"We were talking about the Ranchathon. It's in a couple of weeks," Aunt Eileen added. "And," his aunt looked at him, her expression a tad more serious, "Catherine was telling me she's thinking of keeping the ranch for a summer home."

Washing his hands at the sink, Connor froze a moment, closed his eyes, and without a word, resumed rinsing. Catherine's mind ran off in a multitude of directions. The first and most disconcerting was that Connor found her just fine for kissing in the garden or dancing in the kitchen but not for having around long term. And that stung just a bit, as one of the things that made staying so appealing was the idea of summer evenings, and maybe nights, with the rugged cowboy who had her crushing like a school girl. Whether she wanted to admit it or not, last night when they'd danced in the kitchen and snuggled on the couch with some old movie they barely saw between make-out sessions and tending to

Stacey, she'd felt an aching loss watching him cross the front yard to his old truck.

The only feeling stronger was the anticipation coursing through her this morning at the hope of catching a glimpse of Connor around the house. And maybe even stealing a kiss. Or a hug. Or simply losing herself in his smile. Damn, she had it bad.

CHAPTER EIGHTEEN

"You two are looking pretty cozy." A beer in hand, Finn pointed at his brother Brooks and then took a long swallow.

Brooks glanced over his shoulder to the women sitting on the front porch, chatting and laughing. The scene had become typical at Sunday supper. "Toni and I were going to wait til we spoke with Father Tim, but," a broad grin took over his face, "we're getting married."

D.J. and Connor's booted feet dropped to the floor with a synchronized thud, Finn choked on his drink, and springing forward, Connor slapped his coughing brother on the back and had to snap his mouth shut rather than let his jaw hit the floor.

"Christ," Finn gasped for breath. "I only meant to razz you and then Connor here." Finn swung around to pin Connor with a piercing stare. "Don't tell me you and the brat are getting married, too."

"She's not a brat," Connor spat back.

"Oh, shit." Finn's eyes grew wide. "You're thinking about it."

"Am not." At least he didn't think he was. With each passing day this week he and Catherine had spent a little more time together than the day before. Every afternoon when she came to pick up her daughter, they would stay for supper. Somewhere along the way a new routine was formed of sitting on the back porch while Aunt Eileen and Stacey went through a ritual of doing dishes, then slathering their dishpan hands with lotion. Aunt Eileen, of course, doing all the talking. Outside, he and Catherine gazed at the stars and filled each other in on most of their lives. She'd tried not to cringe at some of the oil rig stories and he resisted the urge to snarl at the retelling of her lackluster courtship with her late husband. They'd gone from her sitting in a rocker and him resting against the railing, to sitting side by side. Last night they'd actually held hands like a couple of bashful pre-teens. He'd loved every second of it.

Even the times when not a word had been said, everything around him seemed better just because she was a part of it. So maybe yeah, he had thought about how it would be to make these changes more permanent. Maybe he had thought about how good ranch life was for Stacey. And maybe he had thought he was a little crazy to be thinking long term with a woman he'd spent so little time with. But so had his brothers. Which brought the conversation full circle. Leaning back, he turned to Brooks. "A little quick on the draw, getting married so soon, don't ya think?"

Still grinning, Brooks shook his head. "I knew she was special the second I saw her hovering over that stupid dog."

Sporting a knowing grin, Adam nodded, as did their dad. The two men appeared to be the only ones in the room not surprised by Brooks' announcement.

"We know to a lot of people it will seem inappropriate so soon after William's death, but we both know *that* marriage was over almost as soon as it began."

Finn set his beer bottle on the side table and shaking his head, pinned his brother with a hard glare. "There's going to be talk. Why don't you wait? It's not like you got her pregnant."

Chair and all, Connor almost scooted back to avoid the icy glare Brooks bestowed on the youngest Farraday brother.

"Watch it." Brooks' chilling stare remained pinned on Finn another long minute before he eased back into his seat. "William's family were barely polite to Toni. I know they were grieving, but anyone could see they'd never considered her a daughter. Part of the family. When the family stood in line to greet the mourners, it was the funeral director who asked for the wife of the deceased and then he had to physically move William's sister out of the way so Toni could stand with the family."

"We get it; the acorn doesn't fall far from the tree. William's family are no better than he was, but that doesn't explain what's the hurry." Finn turned his hands palm up in a questioning gesture.

"If Toni and I are married when the baby is born—"

"You'd be the legal father," Adam finished.

"Exactly."

"Still," Finn let the word hang.

"I know," Brooks acknowledged his brother's concern. "That's why we thought a small service in the church garden, only family. Nothing fancy. She's already had the big hoopla wedding and all I care about is having her and God in attendance. The good padre is just a legal technicality."

"Technicality," Finn mumbled.

"If Father Tim is agreeable, we were thinking Sunday after the Ranchathon."

"That's one week." Connor knew his brother was smart and practical, but right now he had to wonder if he hadn't lost at least part of his mind.

Brooks nodded.

"And you're sure?"

"Absolutely."

Taking a long, hard look at his brother, Connor could see the determination in Brooks' eyes. He also spotted the softness that glistened every time his attention shifted to Toni talking with the other women on the front porch. Connor bobbed his head. "I see." And he did.

"It is what it is. No sense in waiting." Brooks stood. "I'd hoped my brothers would understand, stand with me."

Adam pushed to his feet. "You don't have to sell me. Been there, done that, bought the t-shirt. Love doesn't need a timetable. When it's the right person, it's just right."

The tension in Brooks' shoulders eased. "Thank you."

Finn was next to stand. The kid who had always handled the family as though he were the eldest, not youngest, nodded. "I'll skewer the first person who says anything untoward about my new sister-in-law."

A wisp of a smile touched Brooks' lips as he patted Finn's arm in appreciation. "Thanks. I'm sure it won't come to that. But thanks."

And that left Connor. He approached his huddle of brothers. Slapping Brooks on the back, he nodded too. "I'm in. If marrying Toni next week is what you want, then I'll be there with bells on, standing in line with Finn to protect my new sister-in-law."

First Adam, now Brooks. Both brothers had tumbled head over boot heels in love in no time at all. *When it's right, it's right.* Maybe thinking long term about Catherine wasn't that crazy after all.

● ● ●

From her seat on the front porch, Catherine had a clear view of the men gathered in the living room. From the way D.J.'s chair was tilting forward, Connor sprang to his feet, and Finn coughed up a lungful of air, she'd easily wager that Brooks had just dropped the same bombshell on the men in his family as Toni had sprung on Meg and Aunt Eileen.

For an older lady, Aunt Eileen bolted out of that chair and had her arms around Toni long before Meg had a chance to process the information.

A tiny pang of regret tapped at Catherine's heart. Her and David's decision to marry had been so matter of fact, so expected, there had been little fan fair from friends and family. Yes, there'd been the engagement parties and showers, but no bubbling exuberance or rib-crushing embraces with squeals of delight from their parents. Her father had merely insisted on approving the date to allow for an optimal number of friends and clients to be able to attend. Catherine had known only a fraction of the five hundred guests. And even then only because she and David worked at the firm.

"A week!" Aunt Eileen screeched, catching Catherine's attention. "Lord, woman I may be good, but I'm not that good.

Maybe if it weren't the day after the Ranchathon—"

"We don't want to fuss," Toni cut her off.

"Fuss?" Aunt Eileen eased back a step and still grinning, shook her head. "Honey, a wedding is a thing to be celebrated. Lord knows it hasn't been easy for my boys to find a good woman willing to take them on."

Meg frowned. "How about bad ones?"

Aunt Eileen merely rolled her eyes, and Meg did a pitiful job of biting back a laugh.

"Under the circumstances—" Toni started.

"Circumstances, shmircumstances. No Farraday is going to sneak off and get married because you're bastard—God rest his soul—of a late husband got what he deserved."

Laughter gone, Meg gave her friend a stern look and an agreeing nod. Catherine couldn't imagine what would have happened in Chicago had she up and decided to marry Connor only a month after David . . . *Marry Connor*? Where the hell had that . . . Turning her attention back to the men now slapping each other on the back, laughing, and raising their drinks to each other, her gaze locked with Connor's.

Galloping at the same speed as Pharaoh that first day in the empty field that separated the two homesteads, her heart slammed hard into her ribs. Rooted in place, their eyes remained fixed on each other. The intensity nearly overwhelming. The need to breakaway, rush into the house, and fall into Connor's arms was so strong she physically ached. Dear God, she'd fallen in love with a horseman.

CHAPTER NINETEEN

"**I**s everything all set up?" Aunt Eileen carried another frozen, baked dish from the extra freezer.

Still at the back door, Connor kicked the dust from his boots before crossing into the kitchen. "Yep. Finn's a slave driver. Tents up. Tables and chairs are out. Food tables have tablecloths. Bleachers are up. The Kennedys are unloading the goats. Ramseys brought the sheep early this morning. Calves have ribbons on their tails. Bulls—"

Aunt Eileen set the dish on the counter beside her and raised her hand to him, palm out. "A simple yes would have done."

Connor stopped mid-stride and stared at his aunt. Since when had a simple yes been enough? His entire life a checklist had been standard operating procedures when reporting on completed chores. Granted the annual Ranchathon wasn't exactly a chore, but still.

Plate in hand again, she breezed by him. "Also Catherine is on her way over with Stacey. I thought now might be a good time to let her know what's going on around here."

Before he could answer the screen door had slammed shut behind her. With the town folks due to start arriving shortly, his aunt had just about finished piling the last load of food into the bed of the truck.

For the better part of the week, he'd practiced in his head how to explain to Catherine that her daughter would be competing in some of the children's events. Though he didn't think she'd be too upset with the gunnysack races, he'd had a nightmare or two over how she would react to anything involving cattle and horses. He didn't have a clue how Catherine felt about sheep, and frankly, at this point, he was delighted to have at least one event for which he could draw on plausible deniability.

"Why do you look like someone took the sugar out of your cake?" Aunt Eileen came back through the back door.

"Just thinking."

"About Catherine." It wasn't a question really.

Connor nodded.

She paused to study his face. Most times he didn't mind, but if there'd been a time one of the kids had something to hide, that woman always seemed to be able to read it on his or her face. "Can't tell if you're wavering on how to tell her you've been encouraging Stacey on the animals her mama is terrified of, or whether it's too soon to ask her to marry you."

Connor felt his eyeballs strain from their sockets.

"Put your eyes back in your head. You can't hide your feelings any more than Adam or Brooks could. I swear this last week every time the two of you walked into a room together your father and I were waiting for y'all to self-combust."

Words stuck in his throat. More than once this week he'd wished he had his own place on the ranch or that Stacey had some little friend she could spend the night with. Working on a ranch from before sunup til after sundown and surrounded by family twenty-four seven didn't allow much time for stealing kisses. At least not the kind he'd wanted to share. He'd already made up his mind. After tonight, if Catherine didn't kill him first, he was going to lay his cards on the line. Find out if this thing between them was destined to burn out before she turned tail and ran home, or if she be willing to take a chance on a former oil rig worker and a startup stable. "How do you do that?"

Aunt Eileen sprouted a huge toothy grin. "It's a gift. So which is it?"

"There's no marriage proposal in my mind or anywhere else."

The crestfallen look on his aunt's face almost made Connor laugh. After a moment of silence, she bobbed her head and, turning away toward the freezer, muttered loud enough for him to hear, "Thought I'd raised you boys smarter than that."

"Doesn't anyone believe in dating in this house. Courting?"

"I don't know. Do they?" Meg came in the front door with an armful of trays that Connor was pretty sure were Toni's now-famous cake balls.

"Just mumbling."

"That's okay. You mumble away, but as someone who loves you, I have one piece of advice."

Connor raised a brow.

"All the time and dating in the world isn't going to turn any old person into the right person. When it's right, it's right." She came up close to him, set the trays on the counter, and after placing a gentle peck on his cheek, leaned back and smiled. "And when you find her, you'll know it."

Aunt Eileen came out of the back with another covered dish, and Meg picked up the trays she had just set down. "Toni's bringing some more when she and Brooks come out. Adam's in the barn with Dad, and I'm here to see what you need."

"You're a blessing, Margaret Colleen Farraday."

Meg grinned up at his aunt. She'd blended right in. Even called his father Dad. And apparently had no problem offering sisterly advice either, but she was definitely growing on him. Especially when he saw how happy she made Adam.

Following his aunt out the door again, Meg paused to look at him over her shoulder. "Remember what I said."

Connor chuckled. What had he started? The immediate issue at hand was not his love life, it was how to break the news to Catherine that in a few short hours Stacey would be one of many kids competing for prizes.

"Knock knock." Catherine's voice carried from the front door seconds before Stacey barreled into him. Instinctively, he tugged her up into his arms and laughed when she kissed his cheek. That had been something new, and from the wide-eyed look on Catherine's face, something he probably should have mentioned last night instead of stealing make out moments on the back porch.

"She's been kissing me goodnight for almost a week. Didn't

realize she was sharing the love." If not for the smile on her face and in her voice, Connor might have been a worried at the remark.

"This just started yesterday. I thought it might be a fluke."

In the two weeks since the funeral, Stacey had grown more and more responsive and interactive. And now she was willing to show even more affection. The only thing that still separated her from any kid in town was her perpetual silence. Though he had caught her humming with the horses more often, still no words.

Catherine smiled at Stacey. "We almost didn't come."

"Why?" He set Stacey back on the floor.

Catherine shrugged. "I know it's perfectly safe to be watching everything from a distance. I keep telling myself this is just a glorified Texas picnic with innocuous events like three-legged races, but it still gives me the heebie-jeebies."

Connor patted Stacey's shoulder. "Aunt Eileen is by the truck with Miss Meg."

Without a moment's hesitation, Stacey turned, racing to join the two women.

The screen door slammed shut and Connor turned back to Catherine. "But you came anyway."

Nodding, Catherine blew out a sigh. "If you'd seen the devastation on Stacey's face when I suggested we stay home and bake cookies for Aunt Eileen instead…"

Connor's stomach twisted into a knot. He knew how much the little girl had been looking forward to today—and for how long. The idea that she would have had even a moment's disappointment over not coming made his heart hurt. "I'm glad you decided to come."

She nodded again. "Me too."

And sadly, no matter what his aunt's advice, or his father's or anyone else on the ranch, Connor had no choice but to start praying that begging forgiveness worked just one more time.

• • •

"Can I look yet?" Catherine had her face buried in her hands. She knew she was being ridiculous. She'd gotten better about watching the men for at least a few seconds when the bulls first came out of the shoots, but her heart couldn't take it when one fell off and then that tromping bull came so close to stomping on the poor man. So, for the better part of the bull riding event she'd kept her eyes closed.

"It's perfectly safe," Meg said from her left. When Catherine shot her a you-have-to-be-kidding look, Meg shrugged. "That's what they keep telling me."

"Right." After watching cattle roping, barrel racing, and now bull riding, Catherine's nerves had been through just about all they could stand. "When are the sack races?"

"Folks are already lined up," Toni said from Meg's other side. "As soon as they clear the ring, the races will start."

"I see women down there." The number of folks who had come in for the day had totally amazed Catherine. The trucks seemed to wind up the property and out the gates like a scene from that baseball movie *Field of Dreams*. One of the pastures had been turned into a parking lot, and eventually, the army of arriving people subsided and the competitions began.

"Oh yeah. Adam tells me there's no such thing as sexism on a ranch. Daughters grow up ranching just like sons."

"Which means ranch wives can keep up with their husbands?" Toni asked.

"I guess. I think there's a city girl exclusion. I've heard the guys say Aunt Eileen is really good at opening and closing gates, but she draws the line at actually doing anything with the cattle."

"I can't say that I blame her," Catherine added.

"Oh, look," Toni pointed to the left side of the ring. "There's D.J. and Abby."

"Isn't that Adam with Dorothy's granddaughter?" Catherine was getting better at matching names to faces.

"Yep. That's Becky," Meg confirmed.

Catherine pointed to the couple beside them. "Who's that with

Finn?"

Shading her eyes with her hand, Meg stared a few seconds before announcing, "Kelly. Adam's receptionist."

"Oh my." Catherine pushed to her feet. "Is that Aunt Eileen with Mr. Farraday?"

Meg nodded. "I think it's some kind of tradition for all the heads of family to participate."

"Looks like it." Toni pointed to a spry older couple who had to be pushing seventy. Or more.

Catherine wondered why the hell anyone that age would do anything so dangerous. "I sure hope they don't fall and break a bone."

Toni shrugged. "I know a good doctor. Besides, it's all in fun. Can't live life if you're always afraid of getting hurt."

"Ain't that the truth." Meg nodded.

"Hmm," Catherine bobbed her head too, more out of camaraderie then agreement. There was fear and there was common sense. And nothing about running in a sack race as a senior citizen made sense. Then again, neither the hell did wishing she could run the same damn race with Connor instead of... "Who's that with Connor?"

Meg's gaze narrowed. "That would be Molly Carson. She's rather popular with the ranch hands."

"Really?" Now Catherine really wished she weren't so damn scared of anything that had to do with ranching and animals. Maybe then she'd be the one sidled next to Connor. Even from where she sat, Catherine could tell the blonde was channeling her Marilyn Monroe. Eyes batting, cute smiles, and way too much heaving bosom for Catherine's liking. The thought of marching down the bleachers, across the ring, and shoving Blondie out of the way currently held a great deal of appeal.

The longer Catherine watched Blondie putting the moves on Connor, the more her blood boiled. If she was going to be staying in Tuckers Bluff, even for just the summer, they were going to have to come to some kind of a more solid agreement. Yes, that made perfect sense. Except where would that leave them in a month or two when she had no choice but to return to Chicago? What the hell would she do then? For that matter, what the hell was she going to do about Connor Farraday now?

• • •

How the hell he wound up sharing one leg and a gunny sack with Molly Carson was beyond Connor. One minute she was partnered with Rusty, their foreman, and the next, she was plastered against him as Rusty mumbled something about appreciating a favor. If she'd shoved that cleavage in his face one more time, best damn foreman in the state of Texas or not, Connor would have tossed in the sack.

As it was, they'd barely made it to the finish line when she'd lost her footing, tumbled beside him and conveniently landed on top of him. Those blasted breasts practically in his mouth. He didn't dare look up at the bleachers again and see Catherine's narrowed gaze burning in his direction. He was about to be in enough trouble when the kids' events started, he didn't need to be talking his way out of this one, too. And he most certainly did not want what Molly had to offer.

Even if Molly's shapely curves were enough to entice a saint to sin, he simply was not interested. There was only one woman who held his world in the palm of her hand—and it had nothing to do with the damn ranch or stable. When this day was over, he was going to have to stop pussyfooting around and figure out a way to bring Catherine Hammond around to his way of thinking. Permanently.

"We may not have won," Molly cooed, "but I think the effort deserves some reward."

All the polite retorts were shuffling about in his mind, but somehow he was sure if he opened his mouth, nothing polite was going to come out. Turning to the bleachers he saw Catherine chatting with his current and future sisters-in-law. The second her gaze darted in his direction, he waved his hat at her and strode in her direction. From behind he could hear Molly muttering, "I never." As far as he was concerned—with him—that about covered it.

The closer he got to the foot of the bleachers, the better he could see Catherine's expression. The polite and distant smile told him she'd read all the wrong things into that stupid race.

"Ladies." Brushing the dust from his pants he smiled up at all three women, but settled his gaze on Catherine. "How'd you like it so far?"

"What she could see, you mean?" Meg shrugged at Catherine. "Sorry."

To his relief, Catherine chuckled at her. "It's no secret these big animals make me uncomfortable and frankly, I don't want to see some nice cowboy trampled to death."

"Accidents happen," Connor said, "but not that often. No one takes unnecessary chances."

"Okay," Catherine waved a finger at him "You and I have really different definitions of unnecessary. I don't see a blasted necessary thing about riding on a . . . beast."

"It's fun," Connor shot back.

All our young contenders for the ribbon tails gather in front, the announcer called.

"I'll take issue with that one," Meg interrupted. "We most definitely have different definitions of fun. You'd probably enjoy jumping out of an airplane, too."

He just grinned.

"Oh my God. You have," from Catherine it sounded like an accusation rather than a statement.

Angling himself so he had a better view of Stacey and the kids in the upcoming event, Connor figured it would be his good luck if the conversation served as a distraction for Catherine, because he still hadn't figured out how to break the news of her daughter's participation to her. "Let's just say a little adventure is good for the soul."

Adam came climbing up the bleachers, followed by Brooks.

"Where's Aunt Eileen and Stacey?" Catherine asked.

The two brothers looked at Connor. He shook his head and blowing out a heavy sigh, Adam answered, "They're with some of the other children."

"Oh," Catherine scanned the opposite side of the ring where some families with children were gathered. "I don't want to impose."

"Nonsense," Connor chimed in. "Aunt Eileen is loving every minute of having a kid around again."

Brooks sidled up beside Toni and slid an arm around her waist. "I have a feeling she's going to love having a baby around even more."

"No doubt there," Adam added laughing.

And they're off. Look at those calves move.

Connor sucked in a deep breath, and searched for anything to keep the conversation moving and keep Catherine from looking to the children.

Points are awarded by color. Blue is five points, green is four, yellow is three, pink is two and white is one.

"How'd you enjoy the event?" Adam asked.

"Been there, done that," Meg answered. "Let's just say we city girls have a little more adapting to do."

Slippery little devils. The larger the calf the more the points. Oh and we have our first point maker.

Instinctively everyone turned to the action. Connor searched for Stacey. In a red plaid shirt, she was easy to spot amongst the herd of children scrambling and running and tripping after little calves mooing and doing the same.

"Oh, my," Catherine muttered. "That can't possibly be safe. Even the baby cows weigh a couple of hundred pounds."

No sooner had the words come out of her mouth than one kid slipped and fell and Stacey tripped over him falling face first to the ground. Connor willed her to hurry and get up before Catherine connected all the dots.

Had she been looking at his brothers instead of the huddle of children and calves, Catherine would have seen that same silent urging on both Adam and Brooks' faces. Connor almost fisted a cheer when Stacey scrambled to her feet and took off running after one of the yellow tailed calves. The kid was just adorable in her determination. Lunging forward at the animal who was probably more scared than Catherine, the little girl snagged the corner of the ribbon and it unfurled in her hand. Waving it in the air, ignoring the children and cattle running around her, she spun about searching the bleachers.

Mother and daughter spotted each other at the exact same moment.

"Oh my God!" Catherine whirled around to face Connor just as he smiled at the little girl and tipped his hat to her. "You knew! How could you!"

CHAPTER TWENTY

Bolting over the bleachers like a sports star in a TV commercial, Catherine couldn't get to her baby fast enough. From behind, Connor called her name. He was on her heels, but even with his longer stride, she had panic- and horror-induced adrenaline on her side. Already she could see Aunt Eileen high fiving Stacey as Sean Farraday lifted her up in the air, and settling her on his shoulder, whirled her around as though she were the Stanley Cup Trophy. What the hell were these people thinking?

For our next event, we have the peewee flag races starting with our buckaroos.

"Will you please slow down." Connor's fingers wrapped around her forearm. "She's fine. She had a blast."

"Life is about more than just having fun!" Catherine stopped but jerked her arm away. "How dare you put her at risk like that?"

"She wasn't at risk. She's been practicing for weeks." He extended his hand to her and Catherine bounced back a step.

"*Weeks?*"

"She liked the horses so much. You saw that. They made her smile."

"So did that wild dog. I could have just bought her a damn puppy!"

"Relax." He reached for her again.

She knew better than to let him touch her. Brain cells melted when he touched her. Hell, they started scrambling anytime he was near. "Stay away."

Connor snapped straight, a gesture that reminded Catherine of his military background. Only the look in his eyes was one of pain more than that of restraint. She'd hurt him. Her teeth came down on her lower lip. The battle between mind and heart tugged her in opposite directions. This wasn't about him, or her. "I thought she was baking cookies with Aunt Eileen."

"She was. Some of the time." His shoulders relaxed. "They colored and did puzzles together too."

Catherine had the drawings for proof. Still. "How could you? She's *my* daughter. Her well-being is my responsibility. You had no right."

On her first ever pee wee race our next contestant, five-year-old Stacey Hammond is representing the Farradays today.

It took a second for the announcer's words to filter through the fury racing in Catherine's mind. Stacey and Farraday ricocheted between her ears. Whipping her head in the direction of the single rider at one end of the ring, Catherine's heart lurched to her throat. Red Gingham leaned forward, pink cowgirl boots rocked into the side of the tan colored animal with a flowing ivory mane and sheer terror broke through at the top of Catherine's lungs. "Stacey!"

Tearing away from Connor, Catherine ran once again across the field toward the back of the ring. Her body propelled forward by sheer maternal will, her eyes never left her daughter. The tiny body on the massive horse raced forward faster than Catherine could run. She'd turned the bend just as Stacey leaned left and reached for a flag. Catherine nearly stumbled on her own intake of breath, visions of Stacey tumbling off the horse and under its hooves filling her mind.

"Catherine!" Connor ran up beside her. "Slow down. If you fall and break your neck, what good will you do her?"

Catherine didn't stop. Didn't dare waste her precious breath on words. She had to stop this. Now.

"Catherine," he repeated, still at her side.

Moving ahead, Stacey slowed to stab the flag into another large barrel and hurried forward once again. *Dear God, please don't let her fall.* The same thing happened again, and again. By the time Catherine made it to where Eileen and Sean stood just past the ring exit, she didn't know if she should scream or cry.

"Atta girl!" Eileen cheered.

Fingers between his lips, Sean let out a loud whistle.

These people were absolutely insane. How had Catherine thought they were the epitome of a nice, normal family? The life she'd once dreamed of as a little girl herself.

Stacey grabbed the last flag and the horse seemed to fly toward the exit.

At that same moment, Eileen turned to Catherine, a smile as large as the Texas prairies immediately gave way to wide-eyed surprise. "You didn't tell her?"

Connor shook his head.

"Whose insane idea was this?" Catherine looked up to see her daughter only a few feet away, the horse slowing down. The beast carrying Stacey already shrinking in size as thoughts of her baby safe in her arms quickly washed over the earlier terrifying visions. Still seething, she turned on her heel. "Damn it." Hands fisted at her side, Catherine fought the tears pooling in her eyes. "She could have been killed. She's all I have left! You are never, ever to come anywhere near my daughter again." She spun again. "Any of you."

"Mommy, Mommy look." The horse came to a stop beside her, Stacey waving the flag. "I did it."

Sean grabbed the reins and walked the animal a few steps to a side area. A step stool appeared and, looking as though she'd done this her entire life, Stacey tossed her leg over and climbed down from the horse then threw her arms around her mother's waist.

There was no holding back the tears. Catherine's baby spoke. Called her name. Was happy.

As quickly as she'd thrown herself at her mother she pulled away and ran up to Connor. "Did I win?"

"You did in my book, sport."

"Come on, Stacey." Sean stuck his hand out to her. "We need to take Princess to the cool down area."

"Okay." Stacey eagerly took Sean's hand and followed him and the horse down the walkway out of sight.

Eileen opened her mouth as if to speak, and then looking over Catherine's shoulder to Connor snapped her mouth shut and turned to follow her brother-in-law.

Connor's hand fell on Catherine's shoulder. "I had hoped, but didn't expect it so soon."

The sound of her daughter's voice. The beauty of it. The thrill of it, could not compensate for the risks. "You had no right."

"I'm sorry."

"That doesn't change things. She's so little, that horse is so big."

"He's barely fourteen hands. Small for a quarter horse. Good with kids."

"He's still a beast."

Connor said nothing.

"And what if she'd fallen?" she continued.

"But she didn't."

"She could have! Racing across the ring like that."

"Catherine." Standing in front of her, Connor dared to put a hand on either shoulder. "She was barely at a trot. And she's good. Very good. A lot of kids her age need their parents to still lead them from barrel to barrel. I thought that's what we were going to do, but Catherine," he paused to glance over his shoulder and back, "she's a natural. Your mother would have been so proud."

"Don't you dare bring my mother into this." Something deep down inside of her screamed that he was right, but her mind understood that wasn't the point. "You had no right."

Connor took a step back, ran his hand across the back of his neck, and blew out a heavy sigh before turning back to face her. "It started with a smile when Stacey saw the horses. Like the night she picked up the brush. For a little while she'd come with me before you picked her up to brush and care for the horses. After only a couple of days I heard her humming with the horses. Then I heard her humming in the house when she was drawing."

Catherine had noticed that too. It was one of the many reasons she was hesitant to return to Chicago just yet. The little changes

Connor spoke of had given her a hope none of the best therapists could offer.

"Then she wanted to ride."

"How could you know that?"

"I rode in early one afternoon after taking Pharaoh to check a nearby pasture. She and Aunt Eileen greeted me near the barn. Before I could dismount, Stacey was tugging at my pant leg the way a toddler would when they wanted up. So I put her in my lap. She rocked forward. Pharaoh sensed the motion and took a few steps. The grin that broke out on her face was amazing."

Tears threatened to spill over once again. All of this was so damn far out of her skill set. Horses and cows were big and bad and dangerous and she was supposed to protect her little girl. But because of the big, bad horse her little girl called her Mommy again.

"Catherine," he inched forward and brushed a hand down her arm. "I only wanted to make things better. We don't have any horse therapists around here, but I did some research. They're amazing animals for dealing with trauma victims. More and more returning veterans are receiving equine therapy for PTSD. I knew it was the right thing for Stacey, I just didn't know how to make you see it. I'm sorry I didn't handle this better."

"But not sorry you went behind my back. Not sorry enough to present me with the facts and trust me to have my daughter's best interest at heart. Sorry doesn't cut it." Shaking her head, Catherine pulled back. She needed to get her daughter—her talking daughter—and get away from Connor and the horses and the animals and the sense of betrayal. And maybe once her racing heart came close to a normal rhythm, it would be easier to accept the truth. This wasn't where she belonged, and staying on any longer would only make leaving worse for everyone.

The makeshift speaker system broadcast more mumblings from the announcer. Arguing with Connor and hearing her own pulse pounding furiously in her ears, she hadn't paid a lick of attention until Eileen and Stacey came running toward her.

"It's my turn again," Stacey said as she ran past her mother, dragging Eileen behind her.

Connor scooted around and stood between Catherine and her daughter's back.

"Oh no." Catherine wasn't about to hear anymore lame excuses. "No more horses. No more cows. We're going home. Now."

Next up is our new friend Stacey Hammond.

"No!" Catherine yanked her arm away just in time to see a grinning little boy no more than three- or four-years-old come running out of the area with a man yelling "hold up partner" on his heels.

"Excuse us." A man ushered a waddling pair of wooly blobs through the gate.

What the hell?

CHAPTER TWENTY-ONE

If Connor had ever thought fast on his feet he was going to have do better than that now. As surely as he knew he'd been born and raised in West Texas, he could feel Catherine slipping away.

"What is this?" her gaze followed the waddling animals into the pen.

"That's the next round of mutton busting, and if we don't hurry, you're going to miss Stacey."

"Stacey?" All color drained from her face.

"Relax. Please." He hooked her elbow and tugged her to the other side where she could see over the rail, then pointed to the two little kids standing by a couple of sheep. "Listen to me." He hooked her chin with his finger so she'd turn to face him. "She's very excited about this. She's the oldest of the kids doing it. No matter what you think at first, remember her calling your name. Please."

Slowly he let his hand fall to his side and said a small prayer to any saint that would listen, hoping Catherine didn't bolt over the railing and snatch her daughter out of the ring when Catherine saw what was coming next.

He didn't have to see to know the moment she'd figured it out.

The gasp of breath said it all. "Oh my God. You're trying to kill her."

No sooner were the words out of Catherine's mouth than Stacey lost her grip on the sheep's wool and slid off.

Here we go again.

Catherine tore off around the gate and nearly collided with a bouncing Stacey. "Can I do it again, Mommy? Can I?"

On her knees Catherine shook her head, feeling up and down her daughter's limbs as though unable to believe she wasn't truly injured. "I think you've had enough for one night."

"I'm afraid you only get one turn, partner." Connor mussed the top of her hair.

Catherine's head whipped around and she stared up at him as though he'd suddenly sprouted a second head.

Adam and Brooks ventured up beside them, Meg and Toni at their sides.

"You were just great!" Meg squatted down beside Stacey. "I'm thinking a double scoop of ice cream is in order."

"Chocolate?" the little girl asked.

Meg's eyes flashed a moment with surprise before she stuttered and spit out, "Absolutely."

"Now?" Excitement danced in Stacey's eyes.

Over her surprise, Meg laughed. "Sounds good if it's okay with your mom."

Catherine was still staring blankly at Connor, but breaking away, she nodded at Meg, mumbling, "Yeah, sure."

Connor stood in place as his brothers and their better halves escorted Stacey over to the makeshift ice cream stand.

"I . . . I think I've had enough for one day." Catherine almost stumbled backwards. "I'll collect Stacey, her ice cream, and head back to the house. "

At least she hadn't insisted on going all the way home to Chicago. At least not yet. "She has a pretty voice."

Those words brought a brief smile to Catherine's face and the tension coiling deep inside of him relaxed a tiny bit. "Today has been totally surreal." Her gaze drifted to where Stacey and his family had disappeared in the crowds. "I'm not sure I believe I actually heard it."

"You did. We all did." Connor didn't try to hold back his smile.

"Yes." Catherine hugged herself. A part of her wanted to clobber this man and his family for putting Stacey at risk for weeks behind her back. The other part wanted to wrap her arms around him and find a million ways to thank him over and over for giving her back her daughter's voice. She needed to get away. To think. To make sense of the cascading emotions swirling inside her. "I have to go."

"There's a lot left of the day. There's tons more food coming and there will be games for the kids—"

"Games—"

"Games. Roping and horseshoes and, well, I suppose the goat milking might not be a game exactly."

Catherine rolled her eyes and then glared at him. "You're not kidding, are you?"

He shook his head.

"Has she been practicing that, too?"

Again his head moved from side to side. "No, and she doesn't expect to participate, but we did think she'd have fun learning. All the kids do."

"I just bet." Catherine took a moment to survey the area, the children running around, the sheep bleating, the cows mooing, people leading their horses to and from trailers, her gaze stopping at the ice cream stand. Without saying a word to him she walked away.

● ● ●

Growing up with a strong-willed father and without a mother, Catherine had developed a thick skin at an early age and a will of iron soon after. Her entire life had been mapped out. And she'd followed the plan religiously. Right down to her choice of husband and career. Now the world as she knew it was totally upended.

A few feet ahead, her daughter sat with most of the Farraday clan, licking away at her double-scoop, chocolate cone. The scene was so normal, so typical of a day at a fair, and so not what her life had been the last two years. Her heart danced with sheer joy. "Looks good."

Stacey nodded, her mouth and hands covered in dripping ice cream.

"Soon as your done with that, we'll head home. Clean you up."

The little girl stopped and raised her head. "Then we'll come back?"

A pang of guilt at dragging her daughter away from all the fun pricked a hole in Catherine's plan. "'Fraid not, Sweetie."

"But, Mommy. I don't want to leave yet." She'd abandoned any effort of catching the melting drips.

"It's been a long day."

"No one else is going home." Two years without speaking and suddenly her daughter is a skilled negotiator.

Meg waved her thumb between her husband and herself. "We can see that she gets home later."

"Yeah," Toni added.

Stacey's forlorn look slipped away and a smile took over momentarily before she resumed working on the ice cream cone.

Settling her gaze on Meg, Catherine considered the two women's earlier words. They were, after all, city girls like her. "Will you two," she waved her finger from Meg to Toni and back, "promise me no more riding animals?"

Meg smiled. "Not a problem."

"Absolutely," Toni agreed.

"Promise?" she asked again.

"Promise," the two women echoed.

"I promise too," Connor came up beside her. Without turning, she could feel his gaze boring into her.

"Mommy says I can stay." Stacey tugged on Connor's sleeve with one hand.

Without hesitating, he hefted her up, ignoring the chocolate dribbles, and kissed her cheek. "What do you say, can I have a taste?"

Stacey's head bobbed up and down quickly and she shoved the ice cream at him.

Rather than take a bite off the top, he ran his tongue around the edges, cleaning up the drips. "Thanks, partner."

There was that word again. Catherine closed her eyes and took a side step to kiss her daughter's sticky cheek. "See you later, baby. Love you."

"Love you, too."

Turning quickly to hide the tears welling in her eyes, Catherine relished the sound of the three little words. Desperately needing to focus and think, she took the shortcut across the old path back to her grandfather's house. The twenty-minute walk had been the same route the original Farraday and Brennan wives had used to visit with each other when the barren West Texas life became too much for the city women to deal with alone. Nowhere near as isolated as those women must have been, Catherine understood what it meant to be totally out of her element.

The sounds of the Ranchathon followed her a long way before they melted into the silence of nothing but earth and sky. Clean air and quiet breezes. She could actually hear herself breathe. So different from the hectic noisy world waiting for her in Chicago, and yet so normal for Connor Farraday and his family.

Not a single day in her life could she remember being so unsure of the right thing to do. So completely torn as which direction to take. What to think. Who to believe. Her instincts had never failed her before. But had they now?

Nearly to the house, calm from the fresh air and exercise, she could examine the facts more impartially, without bias. Yes, Connor had gone behind her back to teach Stacey how to ride a horse, and yes, this seemed to be what she needed to come out of herself again, but did the end justify the means? Yes, she feared being near horse, cattle, and other ranch animals ever since childhood, and yes, these massive animals could be dangerous— but did she have any right to impose her fears on her daughter? Was that really keeping her safer? It wasn't like families were losing children left and right from ranch accidents. Hell, more kids probably died from eating chemicals in the home than from falling off a horse.

Yanking open the back door, Catherine marched straight to her grandfather's office. In his seat she could see all the heirlooms and memorabilia scattered about the room. The photos of the ranch through the generations. Blue ribbons from the fair. Even a few of her mom's rodeo trophies.

"Your mother would be proud of her." That's what Connor had said. If she were honest with herself, she'd have to agree. Looking at the smiling faces in a nearby photo of her mother on horseback and her grandparents beside her, Catherine had to admit they would probably all have been proud of Stacey today.

"Hold up partner, wait for me." That father hadn't seen anything wrong with his toddling three-year-old riding a wooly sheep. Both father and son had looked damn proud of the whole thing.

And so had Connor. Even now her heart swelled, almost robbing her of breath. He'd said it so easily, so casually that no one else took note. *"You only get one chance, partner."* That was the second she knew but couldn't admit. None of these people were crazy, and her daughter had probably never been in a bit of danger. Now that she thought back, she could see the horse really wasn't as big as the other animals she'd seen on the ranch, and maybe Stacey wasn't really racing at any speed from barrel to barrel. Connor had done what he did because he cared for her daughter. Truth be told, any stranger seeing his face cheering Stacey on, or licking the ice cream drops from her cone, would have thought him to be her father.

Maybe Catherine was just mad because he was right. She wouldn't have listened to reason. She would have allowed her own fears to cloud her judgment and would have prevented the one thing that would bring Stacey's life back to normal.

"Damn it, Grandpa. Why couldn't you have stuck around a little longer? I don't know what to do. I don't belong here. This isn't my world. But it seems to be Stacey's. How can I take her away? What will happen if we go back to a world that had become only darkness for my baby? And me."

Catherine brushed at the tears dripping down her cheek. Why did this have to be so hard? "Damn it!" Waving her arm across the desk, the family photo from decades long ago went flying to the floor along with a few files yet to be sorted.

"I'm sorry, Grandpa. I just don't know what to do. I don't belong here."

About to lean over and scoop up the mess she'd made, she caught a glimpse of a corner piece of a discolored page sticking out from under the blotter. Tapping the edge and pulling it forward, a glossy old snapshot of her grandparents and her mother on horseback again. This time her mom was much younger. Even younger than Stacey. Curious, Catherine pulled it out all the way, another sheet of paper sliding with it.

Examining the photo more carefully, her grandparents seemed older than the other photos from when her mother would have been that young. Dear lord. This wasn't her mom, it was her. At three she wasn't afraid of horses. She was smiling. And her grandparents were smiling. Her mom must have taken the photo. "I'll be damned."

Still clutching the photograph in one hand, she reached for the paper with the other. Letter of Intent. Scanning quickly, her gaze landed on the two signatures at the bottom. Ralph Brennan and Connor Farraday.

Her eyes darted from paper to photograph at the same time her mind played a mental film reel of Connor and Stacey's smiling faces. "Son of a bitch, he never said a word."

CHAPTER TWENTY-TWO

"We promised." Meg dropped her hands on her hips, elbows sticking out like chicken wings.

"You promised to keep her off animals. No word was mentioned of who would bring Stacey home." Connor knew this might very well be his last chance to talk to Catherine and he was sure as hell going to take it.

"Actually," Toni waved her hands palms up, "she did offer to bring her home later."

Adam smiled. "But she didn't promise."

"That's right." Brooks nodded.

Meg and Toni turned to Connor's brothers.

Shrugging like matching bookends, Brooks smiled and Adam said, "We men have to stick together."

Connor leaned forward and kissed his sister-in-law on the cheek. "I promise I'll mention I had to hog-tie you to snatch Stacey away."

Meg rolled her eyes. "Just go. And you'd better make this right. I like Catherine."

He nodded and hoped to hell he could. All she'd done was leave him to walk to the next ranch and the sense of loss weighed on him. The mere possibility that her next step would be to pack up and go home to Chicago was enough to gut him hollow, leaving nothing but a worthless shell in her wake. If there'd been any doubt in his mind before that Catherine was the woman for him, it was completely gone.

"Ready, princess?" Connor called to Stacey, playing in the dirt with some of the other children.

"Okay." She stood up and brushed the dirt from her jeans then waved to the boys intent on their game. At his side she stuck her hand out to him. "Can I have a hat like yours?"

"Well, it might be a little big, don't ya think?"

She pondered that a second, then shook her head. "No, silly. My size."

"Sure." Walking to the car he shortened his stride to match hers and hoped to hell they'd be here long enough for him to get her a hat.

The drive to the Brennan ranch normally took only a few minutes, but weaving around the parking lot of cars still on the property and the folks backing out and leaving added a few more to the ride. Never one to put off a challenge, he forced himself to stay calm and patient and then, when he pulled up to Catherine's door, wondered if maybe a little more planning might not have been in order. Not that flowers or wine would plead a better case, but maybe it wouldn't have hurt.

"Mommy." The second he opened the back door for Stacey, she'd hurried up to Catherine who was already standing at the front door. "We had so much fun. I met Betty and Mike and Tommy and Sissy. We played with the bunnies and stick horses and we tied calves—"

Catherine's eyes shot upward at him.

"Fake ones," he said quickly. "For roping contests. For the older kids."

"Sounds like fun, sweetie."

"It was!"

"Go on inside and wash up."

Bubbling with excitement, Stacey tore off into the house.

"And change your clothes too," Catherine called after her daughter, then leveled her gaze with his. "I thought Meg was bringing her home?"

"I had to hog-tie her to steal Stacey."

"You did."

He nodded. "Can we talk a minute?"

"Actually, I have something to say too." Catherine stepped back and opened the door wider. "Come on in."

Sucking in a deep breath, Connor took his hat off, wiped his shoes and stepped inside.

Leading the way but rather than going into the living room or kitchen the way he would have expected, Catherine went straight to her grandfather's office.

"Take a seat." She waved a nearby chair and circling the old oak desk, took her grandfather's seat. "I've been doing some more work in here since I came home."

Connor nodded.

"The ranch is no longer the operation it once was." She looked up and waited for his confirmation. "I'm a city girl. I don't know anything about running a ranch, nor do I have any interest in doing so."

Connor dipped his chin, but none of his instincts liked the way this conversation was going.

"Seems there are a lot of people who want to buy this ranch." She held out a stack of papers. "Some pretty nice offers, too." She set the stack aside and kept one page in her hand. "I thought of negotiating this one. "

Now would be a good time to mention his deal with her grandfather, but on the other hand, he didn't want any misunderstanding about his intentions. He wanted Catherine and Stacey to be a part of his life with or without the ranch. It might be a mistake, but he kept his mouth shut.

Catherine eyed him carefully, pushed to her feet, and walking around, leaned one hip on the corner of the desk in front of him. "Your brother's been leasing this land a while."

Connor nodded. Words were not his friend right now.

"Think he'd be interested in buying the land if it doesn't come with the house?"

"Why not the house?" Okay. Maybe some words.

"I thought it would be nice to keep the house. Family ranch and all. Maybe a summer home."

Connor didn't know if that was a good or bad thing. His mind wasn't processing business now; his heart was too busy getting in the way. "You could make it a year-round home."

"Could I?"

For the first time since she sat down he noticed a twinkle in her eyes. Those weren't the eyes of an angry woman about to pack up all her marbles and go home. Taking a huge risk, he stood towering over her. "You could."

"Why would I?" this time a hint of a smile teased at the corners of her mouth.

"Because your daughter loves it here."

"She does." Catherine nodded. "But I'm a city girl."

"Lots of city girls learn to love this part of the country." He put his hands on her shoulders and sucked in a relieved breath when she didn't pull back.

"You mean Meg and Toni?"

"Them too." He took a step closer. "I thought you were growing to like it around here too."

She nodded. And his heart kicked into a fast beat.

He closed the gap between them, standing close enough to feel her heart racing in time with his. "Maybe, with a little more time, I could convince you to give us another try."

"Don't need time."

His heart stuttered, until her hand slid up his shirt. "I thought maybe I'd take this offer."

He glanced down at the page she held between them. From this angle he could barely make out the words but he could see the Farraday letterhead and smiled. "You realize, if you take that offer I come with it."

"I do."

"I like those words."

"I hoped you would."

No space between them, his mouth came down on hers. The rest of his life wouldn't be long enough to have this woman in his arms.

"Mommy," Stacey came rushing into the room.

Connor pulled back, surprised when Catherine's hands

remained draped around his neck.

"Yes, baby?"

"Can I have my own horse?"

Catherine raised a brow at him and, gazes locked, Connor waited a beat to answer. "I think I'm negotiating that now, partner."

EPILOGUE

"Talk about life happening while we're busy making other plans."

"Tell me about it." Connor shook his head and smiled. "Marriage and settling down was the last thing on my mind when I came home."

"And now it's more than just on your mind." DJ watched his brother's face light up as he bobbed his head. By the end of the day, two of DJ's brothers would be happily married and from the looks of it, in the blink of an eye Connor would be joining the ranks of not only husband, but like Brooks—father.

The tiny garden in the back of the old church had to be the most peaceful place on earth. When they were all kids, catching frogs or swimming in the creek after the rainy season was the only place the boys wanted to be. All grown up, riding the far pastures on a breezy spring day always helped remind DJ of what was important in life. Here, on Brooks' wedding day, the green grass, colorful blooms, and his mom's bench reminded him he was damn lucky to be a Farraday. His only regret: that his mother wasn't here to see three of her sons find the loves of their life.

"I bet I know what you're thinking, Declan James Farraday." The only time Aunt Eileen called him by his full given name was if he was in trouble. Big Trouble.

"Whatever it is, I didn't do it."

"Well…Declan." Beside him Connor chuckled and stepped aside. "This is my cue to see what's keeping our big brother."

Rolling her eyes, Aunt Eileen shook her head. "It's a nice name. I'm sorry we didn't call you that more often."

DJ nodded. In the marines he'd been known by most as Declan. In Dallas too. At home in Tucker Falls he was DJ to anyone and everyone.

"Your Mama and Daddy couldn't agree on a boy's D name for all the tea in China." Aunt Eileen kept her gaze on the vine-covered arbor in the corner of the garden. The one Brooks and Toni would be standing under shortly. "Since Daniel was out of the question on account of the *Seven Brides for Seven Brothers* movie, it finally came down to David or Dillon."

Cocking his head, DJ glanced at his aunt. Not once did he remember ever being told that his parents had considered any other name for him.

"Your mama favored David. Sean liked Dillon. Helen insisted it was because of *Gunsmoke*."

DJ had to laugh. That did sound like his father.

"The day you were born they still hadn't agreed on a name. I remember it so clearly. Sean was at one side of the bed, holding your mother's hand and I was on her other side. The nurse brought you in all wrapped up in a blue blanket like a silkworm in a cocoon." Aunt Eileen continued to look ahead and smiled. "Helen unwrapped you slowly and as soon as your arm was free you snatched her finger in your hand. Sean grinned as though you'd ridden a prize bull, my sister nodded, looked up at us and said, Declan James. To this day I have no idea where she came up with that name. All she'd say was one look at you and she knew."

"What are you two jawing about?" Sean and Adam came to stand on either side of DJ and his aunt, his brother Connor returning with a grinning Brooks at his side and Father Tim on their heels.

"Names," DJ answered, watching the joy shining from his brother as clearly as though the guy had swallowed a flashlight.

"You ready?" Aunt Eileen turned to face the second oldest Farraday son.

Nodding, Brooks straightened his shoulders. "Absolutely."

"Good," Eileen dipped her chin. "That's what I want to hear." She turned to face her brother-in-law. "I'm guessing you've taken the time for that man-to-man talk?"

The senior Farraday's brows buckled momentarily in confusion before breaking into a low rumbling laugh. "At this point I think my sons could teach me a thing or two."

Two deep lines formed at the bridge of Aunt Eileen's nose and smothering their own laughter, all the brothers took a single step back.

"Yes, Eileen," their father quickly corrected, a stern expression on his face. "We had a nice long talk."

Connor leaned into DJ and whispered, "About twenty years ago."

"Do you think she's kidding?" DJ asked softly.

Turning his head to see his aunt and father laughing, Connor shrugged. "I honestly don't know."

Brooks stepped around his Father and came up to his brothers at the same moment the youngest Farraday brother came through the church doors. "Didn't think you were going to make it, little brother."

"At least I'm not late." Finn slapped Brooks on the shoulder and glanced around. "Always a good sign when I can get to the church before the bride. They should be coming out any second."

Connor's gaze darted to the doors and back. DJ wasn't sure what to blame for his three older brothers falling head over boot heels in love, one right after the other. Late last night they'd all teased something was in the beer. Adam and Brooks hadn't been too much of a jolt; they were the more stable of the bunch. But Connor? And to an outright city girl? One terrified of horses to boot.

Brooks glanced down at his watch, then up at the doors and over to where his father, aunt, best man and the priest were chatting. Brooks looked as nervous as a long tailed cat in the proverbial room full of rockers.

"Not to be difficult or anything," DJ dared to ask, "but you are sure you want to do this?"

Staring at his brother with enough intensity to melt steel, Brooks didn't nod, or shift, but merely kept his gaze on his brother.

"I'm only going to say this to you once. Ask again and you'll be spitting teeth."

Fair enough. DJ nodded.

"I can't imagine another day in my life without her in it. I don't *want* to imagine *any* day without Toni."

DJ nodded again and his brother's sappy grin reappeared. There was no need for DJ to turn and see what had brought the smile to Brooks' face so quickly. The answer was obvious, but DJ looked anyhow. Toni stood by the French doors, Meg and Catherine at her side, little Stacy in front.

In a simple sleeveless ivory dress that came to just below her knees and a lone strand of collar-length pearls which matched the pearl dots at her ears, Toni beamed. In her hands she held a single red rose to compliment the bud in Brook's lapel. They were the only two with flowers.

The family took their positions. Brooks and Toni facing each other in front of the priest, Adam and Meg on either side, best man and matron of honor. Connor and Catherine stood to DJ's left holding hands and smiling like besotted teens after their first make-out session, his aunt and father stood to his right. The words said between bride and groom came out slow and careful and soft-spoken, befitting the reverent location. Not that it mattered. Everything Brooks and Toni said was reflected in their eyes. Love, caring, and devotion. The three magic ingredients.

Rings and smiles, and of course the anticipated kiss, were exchanged. The melding of mouths lasted longer than DJ was comfortable with. Looking away, he leaned over and whispered into his aunt's ear. "You never said, what did you know I was thinking?"

She brushed against him and without turning her face, whispered. "It's your turn next."

"Not likely," he practically snorted.

This time his aunt angled her head and studied him. "I never asked any of you boys what happened while you were living and working away from home. Don't think I want to know."

DJ nodded. Partly acknowledging her respect of his privacy, but mostly because she was right, she didn't want to know.

Her hand raised up and she ran her knuckles gently along his cheek. "Someone is going to come along and she's going to think Declan is the most beautiful name and she's going to make you forget all the things I don't want to know."

DJ dipped his chin, not so much because his aunt was right, but because somewhere buried inside, the carefree young man he used to be wanted her to be right.

Brooks and Toni broke apart and the small family group erupted in applause. Stacy tossed rose petals at the newly married couple.

Waiting her turn to hug the newest Mrs. Farraday, Aunt Eileen leaned into DJ again. "Maybe keep an open mind about the local ladies. You know we have some lovely young women."

"We'll see." Not that he had any intention of changing what had been the unspoken rule amongst the brothers.

Aunt Eileen twisted one side of her mouth up and recognizing his answer for the stall tactic that it was, she shook her head. "Maybe just keep an eye out for that dog. He, or she, seems to have a better track record at finding good women than any of you."

"Oh come on." DJ laughed softly. "You can't seriously expect some dog to drop a wife in my lap?" He'd said that a bit louder than he'd meant to, but only his aunt appeared to have heard.

"No," Aunt Eileen smiled. Taking a step forward, she looked back over her shoulder. "I'd settle for on your doorstep.

Enjoy an excerpt from

Declan

"The Louisville Slugger strikes again." DJ dropped the receiver into place and pushed back from his desk. "That's the fifth mailbox this week."

Teenage hijinks was one thing, but this was getting totally out of hand. And picking on old Mrs. Peabody. Since her husband died the woman had more than enough imaginary problems, she didn't need real ones. Who knew how often he and his department would have to drive by her house until she found something new to fret about. With only two officers besides himself for the small town and the handful of ranches inside the Tuckers Bluff limits, circling Mrs. Peabody's neighborhood all day—and night—wasn't practical, but he'd do it.

Esther, his dispatcher, stuck her arm out. A single pink message slip dangled between her fingers. "You may want to call your brother back."

"Which one?"

"Brooks. I took the call while you were calming down Mrs. Peabody."

DJ looked at the note on his brother's call. *Says he may have saved your day.* "Thanks." A rustling noise near the front door caught his attention, but his cell phone ringing pulled him back. "PC Farraday."

"If you're coming over, you'd better get here sooner than later," Brooks said quickly. "I'm almost done with Christopher Kelly."

"Christopher?" More movement out front had him moving across the bullpen toward the window. "What about him?"

"Mom brought him in with a broken arm."

"Oh really?" Christopher was about to learn the hard way that Karma was a bitch.

"Yeah. I'm guessing you had another mailbox go down."

Even though his brother couldn't see, DJ nodded. "Mrs.

eabody."

"If you want my professional opinion, looks like this middle on isn't taking too well to all the attention the twins are getting."

"Yeah, you're probably right. I'll be right over." DJ slid his phone into his pocket and shifted toward the scratching sound coming from the front door. He waited, then nothing. Maybe his family was right, he needed a little time off. A break. Tuckers Bluff was no mecca of crime, but sometimes having nothing to do all day was as draining as having too much to do. Though he'd take those long winter days of no trouble anywhere on the horizon and the increased mischief come spring over big city crap any day. Turning to face the indispensable Esther who'd worn a badge long before he'd become a cop, he waited for her to finish her call.

"Yes, ma'am," Esther said with a smile. "I know how you feel." She nodded even though the caller couldn't see her. "You can be sure I'll remind him." This time Esther chuckled. "I don't know if I'd say that." Her head bobbed a few more times before her eyes rolled and then the smile came back again. "Yes, ma'am, you have a better day now."

"Let me guess," DJ shifted his weight. "Mrs. Peabody."

Esther nodded. "You talk to your brother?"

"On my way now." When he stepped closer to the door, another scraping sound drew his attention. Waving to Esther, he took a quick broad step and yanked the door open. "Well."

Sitting on his haunches beside one of the old wooden benches flanking either side of the front stoop, tail wagging, tongue lolling, a dog who had to be first cousins with a neighborhood wolf sat as contented as any family mascot.

"Hey there." DJ inched forward, not sure how long that tail would keep wagging. He was rewarded with a raised paw. "You shake, do you?" Taking his chances, DJ accepted the proffered paw, pumped it once and then scratched the animal's neck in search of a collar or tags. "You must belong to someone. No stray learns to shake." *Wait a minute.* "I bet you're the fellow who has been popping up all over the place."

DJ could have sworn the dog nodded.

"Don't go anywhere. I know some people who are going to want to check you out." Continuing to scratch the dog's neck, DJ pulled out his cell and called his other brother's office. Came in handy having both a people and animal doctor in the family.

"Animal Clinic, how may I help you?" Becky Wilson's jubilant voice came through his phone and made him smile. The kid was always so happy and perky, just the sound of her voice could put a smile on the Grinch.

"I've got someone here for Adam to check out."

"Well, he's not here. Things were pretty slow so he and Meg took off for some shopping in Butler Springs."

"Dang. I've got *the* dog."

"*The* dog?" she repeated. "Oh wait. You mean *that* dog?" Her voice kicked up an octave and now he really smiled.

"I think so."

"Cool! Don't let him go. I'm on my way."

Before he could say another word, the line went dead and he decided the Kelly boy could wait. It wasn't like DJ didn't know where the family lived. He just really wished Christopher hadn't graduated from TPing houses to destruction of private property. There'd be no turning a blind eye or giving the token stern warning.

"Becky's on her way," he explained to the dog. "You're going to like her."

The pooch did that head bob that looked like nodding, and spinning round, leaped up on his hind legs and then coming back down, shifted to the opposite side, giving DJ a better view of what had been nestled under the old bench behind the fluffy dog.

"Don't tell me someone dumped your puppies here and that's what's brought you out into the open." Keeping one hand on the dog's collar, DJ leaned over, grabbed hold of the cardboard edge and slid the box out into the open. For a split second he thought he was hallucinating. Blinking once and then twice, he shook his head. No hallucination. Squatting down, he reached forward. "Son f a—"

• • •

Bolting up from her seat, Becky spun around to face her friend and office manager, Kelly. "Looks like DJ found that mysterious dog. He's got him at the station. I'm running over now."

"Is he hurt?" Like everyone else in town who'd heard about the disappearing dog, Kelly knew some reports had the pup limping. No one liked the idea of an injured animal out on its own.

"We'll see. I'll bring him back. Even if he's not hurt, the poor fellow needs a good home."

"The way he took care of Toni's husband and little Stacey, I'd say he seems to have a protective streak. Maybe your grandmother would like another dog. Now that she lives alone and all."

Becky rolled her eyes, and fished her keys out of her purse. "Don't give her any ideas." Skirting the edge of the counter, she waved at Kelly. "Be back soon."

The police station was halfway down Main Street. Not a great distance in Tuckers Bluff, but under the circumstances, walking would take too long. Riding down the block in her little pickup, she moved as quickly as possible without drawing too much attention. Of course, she had to take a minute to wave at Burt Larson pulling in some sale barrels from the sidewalk in front of the hardware store. No doubt lugging those things in and out all day is how he managed to keep up with the town gossip. Then the small town code of ethics required her to roll the window down a minute to share a word with Polly closing up the Cut and Curl. "Early day today?"

"Yeah, Mrs. Thorton cancelled her color. Figure it's about time I had an afternoon off."

Becky nodded and waved. "Enjoy."

Most of the storefronts rolled up the welcome mat early during the week, and if she'd waited a few more minutes she'd have probably had to stop for every single proprietor making their way home.

For a place intended to contain lawbreakers, the police station had a very pleasant curb appeal. Becky slid into an open spot in front and, scurrying past the benches and potted plants to the inset triple glass door, practically ran inside only to stop short in the middle of the bullpen.

As expected, DJ stood with a better than medium sized furry gray animal at this feet, but rather than waiting for her in his office, the two were completely fixated on Esther, the dispatcher, patting and rocking a baby. "Starting a babysitting service now?" she asked.

"Apparently." Esther hummed to the infant curled into her shoulder.

The dog broke free of DJ's hold and loped in Becky's direction.

"Whoa." DJ turned after the dog.

Tail wagging, the pup reached Becky first, plopped his butt in front of her and offered his paw.

"He did that to me too." DJ stopped in front of her, his darkened gaze darting back to the baby.

"So you're a gentleman, are you?" She squatted down to scratch the dog's neck, then raised her head to look at DJ. ""Whose baby?"

"We were just about to find out."

"Find out?" She glanced from DJ to Esther and back.

DJ waved a couple of envelopes at her. "The baby was left here on the stoop in a cardboard box. These came with the bundle." Turning toward his office, the envelopes in one hand, DJ gestured toward the dog with the other. "Rin Tin Tin here was standing guard."

"Aren't you a good doggie." She continued scratching behind his ears. "I can't believe anyone from around here would just drop an unprotected baby off on the doorstep." Patting the top of the dog's head, she pushed upright and walked over to Esther. "Girl or boy?"

"Haven't checked. When the chief picked the box up, the poor thing startled awake and Mr. Dad over there handed it off to me so fast you'd have thought the baby was on fire."

Cooing, Becky patted the baby's back. "Aren't babies so sweet."

DJ tore at an envelope and walked into his office.

The phone rang. Esther looked over to her boss, shook her head, and handed the baby to Becky. "Someone needs to answer that."

"Yes, someone does," DJ called from behind his desk, whipping the folded sheet of paper open.

Becky followed him in. The dog plopped down at the doorway, his gaze on the front door. Swaying and patting, she rocked the little bundle back to sleep. She loved babies. All children, actually. Ever since she was a little kid herself she'd dreamed of a pretty white ranch house with a picket fenced side yard and small children with those strong chiseled Farraday features, deep blue green eyes, and Ethan's sandy hair. Though with every passing year, the longer Ethan stayed married to the Marines, the less Becky's dreams of happily ever after seemed likely to come true. But she wasn't ready to give up on the one love of her life. Not yet. "Who would abandon something so precious?"

"That's what I'm trying to figure out." DJ continued to scan the page in front of him. "All this says is that the few days she and the father spent together were fantastic." He glanced up over the edge of the page. "I'll spare you the er…intimate details."

Becky looked down in an effort to hide the blush she knew would creep into her cheeks any minute. She could joke and tease about sex with the girls any Friday night, no problem, but surrounded by strong handsome men, or in this case, man, her old fashioned upbringing always came to life.

"Sounds like mama was—is—a bit of a wild child," DJ continued scanning. "Thought maybe it was time to settle down. That getting pregnant even though they'd used precautions was a sign from God." DJ raised his dark brows at that one.

"I'm guessing the novelty wore off pretty quick."

"Yeah." He turned to a second page. "She's just going to drive and stop wherever the bright lights call to her, knows Brittany—"

"So you're a girl." Becky kissed the top of the precious child's head. "I should have known. Such a sweet face."

DJ continued, "She knows she'll be better off with a stable family. Sh—oot." DJ blew out a heavy sigh, and closing his eyes, pinched the bridge of his nose. "Sounds like Daddy Dearest is married. Wonder how well that's going to go over with Mrs. Daddy Dearest."

"Does the letter say who Daddy is?"

Shaking his head, DJ set the paper on the desk and pulled out his cell. "Reed, I want you to park yourself at the mouth of Rte 9."

"We looking for drunks or speeders at this time of day?" the junior officer asked.

"Neither. You see any car you don't recognize, pull the plates and call me back." DJ disconnected the call and continued scanning the letter.

"You think the mother's not local?"

DJ nodded. "We don't have any place in town for a married man to have a long weekend party that his wife won't find out about."

"Why'd she drop Brittany off here instead of with Daddy?"

"Probably," DJ folded the letter back into the envelope and slid out another sheet, "so that she can't be prosecuted. Leaving the baby at a safe house in Texas protects her."

"I don't call the front stoop very safe."

"Yeah, she probably knew one of us would be coming in or out." He looked up through the glass windows of his office and toward the front door. "This is going to be a mess. Even if we figure out who the father is, I'll have to call in protective services, find a certified foster parent. You know the father's going to want DNA tests and unlike TV that sure as hell won't happen over ight."

From all the rocking in place, even with the conversation, the weet baby had fallen fast asleep. Becky shifted her weight. "I can elp."

DJ unfolded the paper and looked up at Becky. "You know omething I don't?"

"No. But I'm certified for foster care. Remember Gran's ousin Gert died while visiting a couple of years ago? She had her randson Chase with her. His mama had been gone a while by then nd she'd never told Gert who his daddy was."

"That's right. Y'all had the boy for a couple of months before ocial Services found the father."

"We'd have kept him too if Gran hadn't liked the guy. pparently he didn't even know he had a son."

"Seems there's a lot of that going around." DJ returned his ttention to the page in front of him. Like a full moon in autumn, is eyes rounded wide until the whites totally surrounded those eep blue orbs.

"What is it?"

His hand fell hard to the table. "This is a birth certificate."

"Good. At least we know who the mother is."

DJ nodded. "We know the father too."

Something in his voice gave her goose flesh. Surely DJ hadn't een the one carousing with strange women. Though now that she hought about it, none of the Farraday men dated the local girls, nd she'd have to be a damn fool to think they were all celibate. he swallowed hard and waited for his next words.

"Becky." He sucked in a breath. "It's Ethan."

MEET CHRIS

USA TODAY Bestselling Author of more than a dozen contemporary novels, including the award winning *Champagne Sisterhood*, Chris Keniston lives in suburban Dallas with her husband, two human children, and two canine children. Though she loves her puppies equally, she admits being especially attached to her German Shepherd rescue. After all, even dogs deserve a happily ever after.

More on Chris and her books can be found at
www.chriskeniston.com

Follow Chris on Facebook at ChrisKenistonAuthor
or on Twitter @ckenistonauthor

Questions? Comments?
I would love to hear from you.
You can reach me at chris@chriskeniston.com

CPSIA information can be obtained
at www.ICGtesting.com
Printed in the USA
LVHW010549301118
598764LV00002B/505/P